FROM AN ALTAR SCREEN

BOOKS BY FRAY ANGELICO CHAVEZ

POETRY

Clothed with the Sun
Eleven Lady-Lyrics
The Single Rose

FICTION

New Mexico Triptych
From an Altar Screen

HISTORY

Our Lady of the Conquest
La Conquistadora: The Autobiography of an Ancient Statue
Origins of New Mexico Families in the Spanish Colonial Period
The Missions of New Mexico, 1776 (with E. B. Adams)
Archives of the Archdiocese of Santa Fe

THIS RETABLO FOR PABLO

FROM AN

EL RETABLO:

Fray Angelico Chavez O.F.

FARRAR, STRAUS AND CUDAHY

NEW YORK

ALTAR SCREEN

Tales from New Mexico

ILLUSTRATED BY PETER HURD

Published simultaneously in Canada by
Ambassador Books, Ltd., Toronto.
Manufactured in the United States of America
by H. Wolff, New York
Design: Marshall Lee

CONTENTS

THE BELL THAT SANG AGAIN, 2

THE FIDDLER AND THE ANGELITO, 22

THE ARDENT COMMANDANT, 30

THE BLACK EWE, 52

WAKE FOR DON CORSINIO, 64

THE LEAN YEARS, 78

THE COLONEL AND THE SANTO, 104

Author's Note, 118

THE BELL
THAT SANG AGAIN

AFTER PASSING ALONGSIDE THE INDIAN PUEBLO THE
road begins to veer steadily to the left, then eats its way
through a huge shoulder of gravel to draw you into a little
valley where everything is red.

The weather-chiseled mesas to the right and to the left
and straight ahead, the uneven ground and jagged arroyos
on either side of the road, are all a deep rouge. Even the
low houses of Santa Ysabel, their adobe walls molded from
the earth about them, seem like chunks broken off the
taller cliffs. The maroon chapel lifts its rounded shoulders

above the dwellings with its windowless haunches to the roadside.

Not until one goes around to the front entrance does the old bell come into view. It hangs, to one side of the door, between two forked cedar posts that frame a delightful picture—a little stream glistening at the bottom of a slope, where leafy cottonwoods on either bank appear greener than usual, the hue of a rare jade, for having a backdrop of reddish cliffs directly behind.

Rather less bell-shaped than the ones hung in the façade

niches of the much older Indian Mission, and though unseen from the nearby road that crosses this out-of-the-way
valley, this bell is not entirely unknown. Some years ago
an enterprising young priest read the date on it as "1110,"
proclaiming it as the oldest bell in the New World, very
likely a stray from some forgotten minaret in Moorish
Spain. Its tone does suggest such a romantic idea, for the
mere touch of one's fingernails sets it to singing sweetly,
belying a legend among the oldest townsfolk that once
upon a time, when it was new, it refused to sing. The people refer to it as "Zacharías," although there is no name
upon it, only the bare date, which a sober reading makes
out to be the year 1770.

The village of Santa Ysabel was founded by a Don
Remigio, whose last name is forgotten, with a number of
poorer families from the overcrowded Rio Grande valley
several miles below to the east. The Indians of the Pueblo
eagerly gave them the land, as the settlers would serve as a
buffer between their town and the marauding Navajos on
the west. They even helped the Spanish people build their
first homes and also their church, which Don Remigio
dedicated in honor of Santa Ysabel, this being the name
of his motherless young daughter.

The choice of title was agreeable to all the settlers, even
if their leader had not sought their voice in the matter, because they did cherish Ysabel sincerely. Not only was she
good, and rather pretty, but she alone among them had a
head of hair the color of clean wheatstraw, that rare strain

of gold running through some of the Bacas of Belen and a few other New Mexico families.

But no matter how much Don Remigio and his fellow-settlers begged the kind Indians for one of their mission bells, bestowed on them a century before by the King of Spain, their friendly neighbors would not part with any of them, not even at a price. So it became a question of making one.

But how? No one in the whole kingdom of New Mexico had seen one made. A man who had been in Santa Fe of late said that there was a new Captain at the Presidio who could do anything, or at least said so. He had already carved a saint for the Indians of Tesuque, or some such Pueblo near the Capital, and with equal skill had repaired some old cannon at the Palace of the Governors. He was a certain Captain Pelayo (no one knows if this was his first name or his last) who had come from the mountains of a place called Oviedo across the sea.

Don Remigio lost no time and had little trouble engaging the services of Captain Pelayo, who arrived at Santa Ysabel one day with a heavy bundle of jagged bronze shards, the relics of broken ordnance pieces of long ago. The red-headed Captain also brought his handsome smile and bearing, and an endless string of stories which he trippingly unraveled in a faultless Spanish that enchanted every one of the village women from the beginning.

Young Ysabel, who was already married, was the one charmed the most. It happened that she had been solemnly betrothed to a youth named Joaquín Amaya before they left their old homes by the Rio Grande. The new church of Santa Ysabel had witnessed the settlement's first wedding, shortly after being roofed, when Joaquín and Ysabel plighted their troth forever at the aged hands of Father Bartolo, the Franciscan Padre who lived at the neighboring Pueblo with his Indians.

And so, Joaquín Amaya was visibly annoyed from the start by the glances which Captain Pelayo cast on Ysabel whenever she and other women, on their way to or from the river with water-jars on their heads, loitered awhile to watch the progress of the primitive foundry which the men were building under the Captain's direction. The young wife unwittingly added fuel to the fire when at table, or after they were in bed, she remarked to Joaquín how clever and gallant the Captain was.

As the work went on, the other men also came to dislike him. Their easygoing natures were irked by his brisk way of ordering them about, but this they would have overlooked since he was a man of arms used to commanding; in doing so, however, he let fall occasional slurs about their own unlettered speech, or about their humble blood which they deemed no less pure than his own. If they persevered in silence, it was because of their single purpose of having a bell in their village.

The day for the casting of the bell arrived at last. Captain Pelayo had fashioned a clay mold which, tightly packed in sand, lay buried in a hole dug in the hard red ground before the church. Close to it stood the foundry, where the molten bronze stirred, impatient to be poured, while the sweating men took turns at pumping a huge rawhide bellows which kept the charcoal fires burning at white heat.

It was then that the Captain, smiling and bowing to the whole village gathered around, suggested that the ladies drop in their most cherished jewelry. This would give the bell its real sweetness, he said. Precious little gold or silver was known to exist among these poor people, yet several of the women ran home and returned to drop in little crescent ear-rings, or tiny crosses and medals with their chains. One housewife, known by all to be very poor, dropped an articulated little fish of pure gold that sank like a released minnow into the bubbling pool. Everyone gasped at the sacrifice of an heirloom that had been treasured, for generations surely, in dire poverty. It was the greatest gift of all.

Deeply moved, Ysabel stepped forward, slipped her wedding ring from her finger, and let it fall into the molten metal.

Those who knew about Joaquín Amaya's feelings, and looked towards him at this moment, saw his dark well-formed features become distorted and darker still. Fortunately, his father-in-law happened to be standing near to him. Don Remigio's hand pressed hard on Amaya's shoulder, and in this manner the older man walked him away from the crowd into his own house. A frightened Ysabel followed them, alarmed by the thought that she had heedlessly done something that did not look quite right.

Her fond father told her as much, though he understood her motives perfectly. This he began to drive into her husband's sullen head, and for this reason they failed to attend the bell's casting. The metal was poured while Don Remigio was clearing two young hearts of all misunderstanding and casting them into a single sound one again. Joaquín loved his wife too well not to be brought to reason, but the fire within him was not put out altogether. It could not be until that arrogant stranger went back to his garrison and soldiers in Santa Fe. That day could not come soon enough.

Captain Pelayo stayed a few days longer for the metal to cool off completely before the bell could be taken out of its buried cocoon and hung up between the waiting cedar posts by the church door. On that eventful morning, Joaquín and all of the townsmen, who had not spared themselves to see this day, vied with one another in helping to hang the bell. Holding their breath, as everybody else did, they watched the Captain approach the bell with a stout iron rod in his hand. He raised it with a look of concern on his now serious features. Then he gently tapped its virgin lip.

The melodious answer with its humming overtones brought a cry of glee from every throat. Every single inhabitant wanted to make it sing; and the bell sang for every one, quite audibly even for babies in arms who patted it with their little palms. What joy there would be this evening when Father Bartolo came from the Pueblo to bless it, and the new town of Santa Ysabel banqueted in its honor under the stars. The Indian chieftains who were invited to the feast would then learn how much more sonorous was this bell than their old weather-beaten ones, no matter what their royal origin.

Wine, a rarity in the settlement, flowed glitteringly that night along the narrow tables set around the little plaza, which was lit up by the fires of barbecue trenches in its center. Don Remigio had bought several skinsful in Bernalillo for the fiesta. He had also slaughtered a fat steer, while the heads of humbler families had killed some lambs and kids to join it in the flaming pits. There were also roasted ears of green maize from the lowlands downstream, and shells of broken squashes sprinkled with brown sugar simmering next to the meat. On the tables were heaps of tart wild plums plundered from the thickets by the river. There were great brown loaves of bread that had been baking during the day in the beehive adobe ovens by almost every door.

Old Father Bartolo blessed the bell before the feasting started. The blue haze of fragrant piñon smoke hovering above the barbecue, and blending at times with the faded blue of his friar's robe, helped to etherealize him in the eyes of his attentive flock as he commended them for their spirit. Though not as eloquent as the Captain, he spoke of wonders closer to their hearts, of truths not merely across the sea but beyond the edge of the world and of time, which were wafted back into the center of their lives and their forgotten corner of red earth.

Even his homely puny face looked comely in the flickering light as he spoke about the famed sweet-toned bells of Bethlehem, at the Franciscan convent of the Nativity where he had served as a young priest, adding that they sounded no sweeter than this humble one which their faith and labor had just brought into being. After describing the ancient chapel at Ain-Karim, the town where Santa Ysabel had lived, he assured them that the adobe church they had recently erected to God in her name was no less pleasing to their Saint.

The entire Holy Land spread around them as he compared its countryside with theirs.

The Padre broke the spell to sit down and partake of a choice slice of beef and some wine with Don Remigio, then took his leave on his little grey donkey. For Padre Bartolo would not ride on horseback. And Don Remigio, whose pious gallantry would not allow the Padre to return to the Pueblo unescorted, mounted his readied horse and left with him. Then everybody, except the women serving, sought a place at the tables.

Over the loud talk and laughter could be heard the singing of the new bell, which the young folks gave no rest, and which their elders did not mind. For the sound regaled their ears as did the food and wine their palates, long starved for delicacies, as the mist of piñon-scented smoke of the barbecue pleased their nostrils.

After a while the men of the town, drunk more with the feeling of having brought an unusual undertaking to a happy close, yet not unaided by a heady wine to which they were not used, grew noisier and more sentimental by the minute. They forgot any hurt feelings which Captain Pelayo might have aroused during their long days of heavy toil; they even paraded him around the square on their shoulders, while the women clapped and shouted for a speech in the alluring accents they had not wearied of hearing. Back at his place of honor, the Captain stood up and thanked the absent Don Remigio for the generous pay received from him, then praised every single man for his share in their uncertain venture, for he now admitted with a triumphant smile that this was the first bell he had ever made. The men stood up and drank a toast to his daring genius. Captain Pelayo in turn offered a toast to the women who had fed them so well, and those foremost who had deprived themselves of their few gold and silver heirlooms, to which, no doubt, the bell owed its delicate sweet sound.

In raising his cup he bowed gallantly to Ysabel Amaya.

Joaquín Amaya smashed his cup on the table and stood up in a silence that swept down the long tables to the last tinkle of crockery at the far ends.

"My Captain," he started out blackly. "We men of the village worked hard under you, even when you insulted our humble ways and our poor manner of speaking. We did it for the sake of the bell."

With one low murmur the men shifted their feelings around the speaker and glared as one armed camp at the Captain, who now stood bewildered and alone.

Joaquín went on: "But my honor forbids me to forgive your latest insult cast at my marriage bond. *Señor*, if you have any honor, you will follow me."

With this Joaquín straddled off his bench and walked away toward the sloping path leading to the river. The Captain met the stares of the other men, as if counting them. Don Remigio was not there to argue some sense into them, and any excuse or apology on his own part would be taken for cowardice, which as a soldier he could not allow. With a shrug of his shoulders, he walked off after the challenger.

Rooted to her place, Ysabel saw her husband's tan buckskin leggings and breeches disappear in the dim edge of the firelight down the slope, then his white cotton shirt and his black tousled head. The vision was repeated with the scarlet artillery hose and gallooned velvet pants of the Captain, then his white cambric shirt and his chestnut hair. A picture of the sharp knives which both men wore in the front of their sashes came to her next. She stood up with a little whimper, then ran after the two men.

Her scream of terror, when she reached the top of the slope, brought the entire village running after. Down below on a sandy flat next to the stream could be seen two prone white shirts. The men hurried down to find Joaquín with a military dagger completely buried in his throat, while next to him lay the Captain with a hunter's knife pushed deep under his ribs. It must have happened at the very first rush in the dark, the left fist of each not fast enough, or strong enough, for each other's right arm.

Their white shirts were fast becoming a glossy dark, but the men feared to remove the weapons, knowing from experience how all the blood would spill out in one fast rush. Without waiting to be told, some young men set off at a gallop to fetch the Padre.

Father Bartolo's slow burro had not plodded further than a mile, with Don Remigio's horse pacing it impatiently, when they were overtaken by the spurred swift ponies. Tightly clutching Don Remigio's middle from behind, the Padre hastened back on horseback and soon had the dying men reconciled to each other and with the Lord.

Don Remigio half-carried his daughter, limp and dazed, back to his house, surrounded by the wailing wives of the village. But as they passed the mute bell in the dimming light of the dying barbecue fires, Ysabel stopped short and stood up stiffly. They all heard the words she slowly and bitingly aimed at the bell, all the more awesome for coming from lips that had never uttered anything so harsh.

"My curse on you—you cause of my sorrow!"

A strange thing happened the next day when they began tolling the bell at the funeral of the two slain men. Instead of singing, it gave out a dull dead sound, like one of the royal bells at the Pueblo which had a crack up and down its side. But, close as they looked and tested, they could find no signs of cracking in the new bell. Therefore, they concluded, it must be the curse of Ysabel on "the cause of her sorrow."

Worse still, when the ungodly sounds reached inside Don Remigio's house, one of the women attending Ysabel rushed out to make the tollers leave off striking the bell, for the noise was driving the girl wild and frantic. Then and there Father Bartolo gravely decreed that the bell must not be rung again until Ysabel recovered from what he termed her disorder of soul. Some of the people were for burying the thing in the pit where it had been born, but Don Remigio's wiser counsels prevailed. A silent bell was better than none at all; for rare was the Spanish chapel that could boast of one, as the Crown had sent bells to the Indian missions only.

For weeks Ysabel sat in a corner of a bedroom in her father's house. Often he came to see her during the day. The old *genízara* woman who kept house for him brought in her meals, which she coaxed her to eat at times. Other women of the village would come and sit by her, to exchange whispered talk among themselves since she ignored them completely. Wise in women's ways, they saw certain signs on her, early but sure, which they relayed to Don Remigio.

The welfare of a future grandchild, for which he had prayed in happier days, made him all the more anxious about his daughter's disorder of soul, as the Padre had put it on the day of the funeral.

Ysabel, however, was not unaware of what was being done for her. But even when she was hungry, she resented the old woman's dumb efforts at feeding her. She dreaded her father's entrance into the room because the pious phrases ever on his tongue made her very insides rise with bitterness. When Father Bartolo came on a visit, and talked about things she had often heard him utter at Mass, she felt like laughing him to scorn; she even wished to tell him to straighten his eyes, for the old Padre was so wall-eyed that the people used to say that he had one eye on heaven and the other on whatever he could get on earth.

But at night, dark nights when she tossed about on her mattress, to fall asleep at last out of sheer weariness, but never to rest, she felt sorry for the old woman across the room who stayed awake most of the night only for her sake. And the kind wives who left their heavy housework and their children to tender her some comfort, whom she ignored and despised for being such slaves to their daily drudgery, how she yearned to hug and kiss every single one. She sobbed painfully remembering how during the day she had caused her father so much anguish, a man so good that the Lord Himself must respect him the way the village folk did. As for Father Bartolo, she was shocked for having inwardly mocked the saintly old fellow, whose crooked eyes his flock made fun of, true, simply because they sincerely loved him and knew that he did his duty without hope of earthly reward.

Yet, when morning came, it began all over again, that dullness in her eyes and mind, that tightness in her throat and breast, that bitter anger against everything and everyone that must end sometime, or else wring the very life out of her, a thought that bore a perilous hint.

This wretchedness of being all alone, in spite of the

efforts of loved ones to enter and share her sorrow, could not be borne much longer.

It was already October, the night Ysabel sat up alarmed in bed, certain that she would not sleep at all. And the morning was so far away. The old woman across the room was snoring away peacefully, for the day had been a heavy one, what with all the corn-husking and the feeding of the hired help. Her father in the next room, she sensed, was just as tired and as soundly asleep.

She dressed in the chill air of the room and stepped into the kitchen. There she removed her father's cape from a peg by the door, threw it over her slight shoulders, and went out into the cold harvest night.

With but a glance at the church and the bell, both well outlined in the moonlight, she took the path leading down toward the river. For a moment she paused to stare blankly at the soft sand along the bank, then stepped across the stream over the outcropping stones, for the water was always low in the fall. Last spring, Joaquín had to wade knee-deep in the swift current while she let out screams of mock fright in his arms. From under the gaunt leafless cottonwoods, bone-white in the silver light, she started up the opposite slope, following a goat-path that led steeply up through a break in the cliff onto the flat top of the mesa, where the dry grama grass shone almost white and the small clumps of juniper looked like dark cattle feeding.

But Ysabel turned right, along the rim of the cliff to a point where it dropped straight down. She had been here before, with Joaquín during strolls both before and after their wedding, even as late as the Sunday afternoon before the bell was cast. How Joaquín had laughed because she was afraid to come near the brink and peer down. If he could only see her now, standing alone and upright at the very verge, looking down at the white beckoning fingers of the cottonwood limbs far below and the thin sheet of water among the stones that reflected the moonlight like a broken mirror.

By spreading out her arms, and the mantle, she would be able to skim down like a hawk, softly and swiftly, and then not feel anything at all . . .

Suddenly she knew that she was not alone.

Someone very near had just touched her. It was like a sweet gentle kick. There it was again, another little kick beneath her heart. A feeling such as she had never felt before flowed up from her fainting knees to her breasts and up along her throat. Slowly she backed away and sank into a natural bench of sandstone blocks that half-tripped her, inviting her, it seemed, to sit down.

"I am not alone any more," she sighed, wonderingly, to herself.

"No, my child, you are not alone," she heard another voice say.

Looking up, but not startled, Ysabel saw an old, old woman seated beside her. She looked like a grand-aunt she remembered as a little girl back in the Rio Grande valley, but her face was youthfully pretty in spite of the many wrinkles. The moon seemed to have gotten brighter, if only to bring out the details of the visitor's features and her plain dress of grey calico, and the black fringed shawl that all the old women of the region wore.

"You are so kind, *señora*, to come," said Ysabel, full of a wonderful trust. "Do you live near here?"

"Yes, dear Ysabel, I have a house down in your village. Your father had it built for me. I come there often. To-night I came because I heard the child leap in your womb. I once had a child who kicked me for joy when the Mother of my Lord and her unborn Son came to me."

"Then you must be Santa Ysabel!" the young woman cried, not too much surprised to find herself sitting next to St. Elizabeth, the mother of John the Baptist, whose story Father Bartolo had so vividly painted when the church was dedicated, and lately touched upon at the blessing of the bell.

"But you must be cold up here on the mesa with only that thin shawl," she continued. "This my father's cape is thick and warm—and, oh, here are his tinderbox and flint in the pocket. I shall make us a little fire."

There were many bits of dry juniper twigs strewn about on the ground nearby, and strips of cast-off bark. With these and bunches of dry grass, she soon had a small fire kindled on the flat rock-cap of the mesa rim where they sat. As the old lady put out her thin brown hands to warm them, her shawl slipped down to her thin shoulders, baring her finely combed white hair that caught the moonlight like a halo. Then she took out a rag pouch from the depths of her ample skirt, and began pouring some thin flakes of native tobacco on a neatly cut piece of cornhusk. When the cigarette was ready, the young Ysabel drew a burning stick from the fire and helped her light it, and the old Ysabel took a few puffs in silence, just like the old women in the village, shielding the glowing end in the cup of her left palm while she propped up the bent elbow on her right hand.

"I did not know that you were so old," Ysabel spoke at last, snuggling comfortably against her shoulder. "Tell me about your boy. Father Bartolo says that there was no greater man born than he."

"My John was called great even before he was born. I was old, too, when I had him." Here she chuckled. "Zachary, that was my husband, would not believe it at first. He was actually struck dumb. These men . . ."

The old lady did not finish the sentence, pausing to take a few puffs in pensive silence. Finally, she spoke again.

"Well, John grew up and went into the desert, something like this place up here. In fact, all this is very much like the hill-country where we lived, Zachary and I. This is another reason why I love to come here once in a while."

Ysabel recalled that Father Bartolo had likened New Mexico to the Holy Land.

"John's work was to prepare the way of the Lord by calling the people to the baptism of repentance, telling them how the Saviour to come would baptize them with the Holy Ghost and with fire. Later, my poor John was killed."

Ysabel now thought of Joaquín. "And so you lost him."

"Oh, no, my dear child. I gained him. For I was already gone from this red earth."

A question that had bothered Ysabel since they moved here from the Rio Grande now came to her mind. "And why is this earth red?"

"The entire earth is red, my dear, red with blood and pain. It is red with the blood of women when they are not having children, and also when they do have them. And it is red with the blood being shed by men through wars and crimes. Bloody noses when they are children, bloody heads when they are grown. In John's day, the king had taken his brother's wife, and my John reproved him for it, and so his head ended up on a blood-stained platter."

The girl was weeping softly to herself, because of the foolish and needless thing that Joaquín had done, and the Captain, all for the sake of a trifle they called honor, not for God's own right. But she now felt a glowing warmth entering her whole being, for she knew that she had always been faithful to Joaquín. Though she had admired the handsome Captain, not once had she flirted with him, not even in her heart.

"Hearts will ever bleed upon this red earth, my daughter, even the innocent. Why? I myself know it now, but you would not understand if I told you, only darkly . . ."

The old *genízara* in Don Remigio's house had awakened with a start to find Ysabel gone from her bed, and had seen the light on the mesa as soon as she opened the kitchen door. Soon Don Remigio and several men were climbing the rocky goat-path to the crest of the bluff.

They found her sitting upon a large stone, her head and back resting against other square boulders. She was sound asleep, and there was a faint smile on her lips. The little fire was almost out. Tenderly, her father picked her up and carried her back home with a heaviness in his breast that was not relieved until morning, when Ysabel, though weak and suffering from a cold, showed in many ways that she was well again.

Week followed upon week, and one day a man-child gave out his first lusty cry in the house of Don Remigio. When Father Bartolo came from the Pueblo to baptize the baby, Ysabel told the Padre that his name would be, not Joaquín or Remigio as he suggested, but *"Juan."* She also asked him to have the bell rung, and at the end of the ceremony, when they struck its sides, the bell sang out again sweet and clear, as it had done the first time and as it has done ever since.

Ysabel, her bed pushed to the window from where she could see the godparents come out of the church and pause by the singing bell, laughed happily and told the good women preparing the christening feast that the bell's name must be Zachary—for did it not belong to Santa Ysabel?

THE FIDDLER
AND THE ANGELITO

FROM HIS FATHER FACUNDO HAD INHERITED A
creaky old violin and a paunchy female burro, together
with a log *jacal*, plastered with the clay from which adobes
are made, and which sheltered both the heir and the heirlooms.

With these he had also received enough skill to fiddle a
few squeaky tunes and to arrange a cord of neatly-chopped
firewood in the shape of a turkey's spread fan around the
low sides and back of the donkey. With the pardonable
pride of a specialist, Facundo would drive his load to some
kitchen door and, having made a sale, would deftly pull a

rip-cord which allowed the wood to roll gently into two neat piles on the ground.

For years and years Facundo had plied his trade of *leñero*, chopping and splitting piñon and juniper branches as evenly matched as matchsticks, then goading his seemingly overladen burro down the steep slopes of the mountain to the housewives in the valley who knew him as an old man when they were girls. His beast of burden, of course, was the same one only in the sense that one generation followed another from the original stock on the maternal side.

The violin, since it consisted of barren dead wood and the dried entrails of sheep, was the very same one his father had used. Like his father before him, Facundo was never known to play it at home, nor would he consent to fiddle at dances, even those given on the eve of the valley's patron saint.

Only when a child died did he take out the instrument from an adze-hewn chest in the corner of his *jacal.*

Incidentally, it was the only occasion, outside of Sundays and fiestas, that the donkey dam got a rest or the leisurely chance to wander off and possibly assure herself of a successor.

Facundo played long and heartily beside the little white coffin at the home. The melodies were the same *seguidillas* played at dances, half-sad and half-joyful as are old Spanish airs, and nobody wondered about this, possibly because disappointment stalks the dance floor and happiness surrounds a child, even a dead one. How the old fellow kept his flowing beard from tangling in the bow or the strings was more a source of wonder to the many children who hovered about undismayed by death. He then accompanied the body, sawing away all the while, from the home to the mission chapel and from the chapel to the *campo santo*, which lay tilted with its broken crosses and half-sunken graves upon the long bare slope between the village and his own mountain slope.

Such a monotonous life, bleak like a surrealist painter's limitless plain with hunched dark figures in the foreground, had to have a break, a highlight—either a bright pink seashell or a figure in unadulterated zinc white, to give finality to that maddeningly endless plain.

So here is one of those tales which change in name and locale with each telling; in truth, the various narrators in widely-scattered parts of New Mexico will say that it happened to a long-dead relative, or that the said relative knew the old woodcutter and fiddler, whose name was Miguel or Juan or Benito, and who had a tiff one day with an angel.

One summer day Facundo (which is the name I give him) was summoned to play for a little boy who had just died. He had expected the call because that very morning the mission bells down in the valley had chimed wildly and long for pure joy.

For New Mexico folks in those hard times long ago had their Faith for undertaker: a child in his innocence, was he not made part of God's singing Court? Indeed, it was only with regard to children that they were certain of salvation. The complex interior workings of adults, God knows, were for no man to judge, no matter how virtuous a person or how wicked. A grown individual was not even sure of himself in this matter, hence the grim necessity that some men felt for bloody penances at the *morada* during Lent; and one had to beg God's mercy on the most sincere and fervent *Penitente* after he was dead.

But for children who died, reaching Heaven was as simple as passing from one room to another. And so they called them *angelitos*, little angels. And no matter how painful, how bitter, a young mother's parting with the life of her life may be, still the church bells must rejoice that there was another being joined with the angels to praise God forever and pray for his own here below.

In this particular valley, besides the joyous ringing of bells observed elsewhere, there was this custom of long standing which Facundo and his fiddle were carrying on. But this time he received the news with a bit of impatience. Howsoever even the tenor of his ways and his calling, the old man had a mind of his own, which balked occasionally, and for no reason that he might have given, just as his burro sometimes chose to halt with its load on a steep mountain trail, or shook off the wood before her master had finished his turkey-fan arrangement. Most likely he had contracted this quirk from the animal, wooden stubbornness being an inborn trait peculiar to the species.

Briefly, Facundo told the messenger to be off, that he had decided to fetch wood from a certain cedar clump that day, and that no dead baby was going to keep him from it.

With more than his usual slow purpose he placed the criblike wooden saddle on the burro's back, cinched it tightly under the somewhat swollen belly, and ended this bit of harnessing by buckling the wide strap which passed loosely around the animal's buttocks under the tail. Then, with the authority of a bearded mahout, he gave the word to proceed.

No sooner were they among the pine trees and beyond

sight of the *jacal* than the beast halted dead in her tracks. There was a steep wall of granite on the right side of the narrow path, and on the left a deep arroyo. Facundo stopped to venture a thought, for this donkey had never balked before when not loaded—none of his dynasty of donkeys ever had through the years. When almost buried beneath the fan of faggots, yes; often they halted stubbornly and he was forced to use his stout stick of scruboak without mercy.

He now applied the goad from all angles. Repeatedly the cudgel fell on one side of the rump, then the other. He vainly tried to reach the overlarge bulk of head in front where the great ears were spread meekly outward.

But in his anger Facundo had failed to take note of their position; for in a true orgy of stubbornness those ears either stood up straight like a jackrabbit's, or collapsed stiffly like a pair of scissors against the wooden neck. More blows fell on the end nearest him, accompanied by hoarse threats that echoed through the narrow defile.

Facundo stopped at last; to catch his breath, it is true, and also to find a way of getting past the gray woolly hulk to where the head was attached. For he knew that burros, like more rational creatures, are more amenable to persuasion when the matter is brought before their nose.

At this moment the sound of a thin clear voice gave him a start. He listened, and the ever-soughing pines seemed to hold their breath also.

"You cannot make her go, Facundo," he heard the voice say once more. "I have her tightly by the nose!"

A red cave appeared in the middle of the woodcutter's matted whiskers as his toothless jaw fell. He tried to look over the donkey's head between the massive ears, but it was too far forward. Then he threw his rheumy gaze over either side of the bulging gray flanks, but it was impossible to see around curves.

"You will have to make her back out," said the voice. It was a child's voice.

"Facundo, pull her back off the trail and then go to your house and get your violin!"

Facundo squatted down slowly and peered through the animal's thin legs. Peering back at him stood a beautiful little boy who did not have to bend much in order to look between the forelegs. He still had his little fingers clamped in the burro's nostrils, which as a rule never hung too far off the ground.

His slow mind still unaware of the truth, Facundo began to threaten the boy.

"You ill-reared brat!" he said angrily. "Let go of that nose."

The lad smiled back and did not move.

"If you do not let go of that nose, I will come over and break this stick on your legs," Facundo threatened.

The boy looked at the cliff on one side, then at the gully on the other, and then peeked back beneath the burro with a bigger smile.

"Very well. If you do not let go, I will go and tell your mother."

This time the child's answering smile was absolutely beatific.

"All right, you little *bribón!* Who is your mother?"

"My mother was that woman whose little boy died this morning!"

Slowly it all dawned on Facundo. But when the full truth finally lighted up his brain it was like a sunburst. Still blinded by it, he made the burro back out of the narrow trail by hauling on the loose strap under her tail, and quite smoothly, for presumably the little lad in white was applying his influence at the front end.

When the donkey turned around on wider ground Facundo did not see the child any more, nor did he expect to. But he did recognize the little face in the white coffin down in the valley as he falteringly rubbed the pine-resin on his bowstrings.

And never again did he miss a child's wake or burial; after that, no one had to be sent to call him from the mountain. The joyous peals of the bells below were summons enough.

THE ARDENT
COMMANDANT

IF PRETTY DOÑA CASILDA DE BACA Y SOTOMAYOR is still remembered after some five generations, it is because of the nature of her amorous adventure one winter's night, and not so much the antique landmarks and objects, or the historical personages, connected with it. Yet these other matters cannot be ignored; in fact, they have to clutter up the tale, like so many stakes holding a great tent taut and fast, otherwise the whole story flies off madly into space.

In those days the eastern flank of the Santa Fe Plaza de Armas was a single long wall of rounded adobe pierced

here and there with some small windows and doorways. Actually, it was made up of three large old dwellings joined shoulder to shoulder with no inside approaches among them. Each had an enclosed patio, once cheerful with the noises and smells of family life pouring from the four surrounding walls.

Now the first quadrangle, the one closest to the Palace of the Governors, was a customs house with one room serving as living quarters for Captain Salazar. He was in charge of duties whenever a traders' wagon train arrived from Chihuahua or, less often and against royal law, from

New Orleans. The house on the other end was a gloomy store owned by a Canadian whom everyone called "The Frenchman."

In the middle, the house since the Reconquest of a family that had produced no males in the past generation, lived Doña Casilda in a solitary splendor not evident from without.

For she had inherited not only her father's house and the heirlooms of the past hundred years, since the great Reconquistador De Vargas had laid out anew the Plaza de Armas and assigned the choicest lots fronting it to favorite captains, but she owned five well-stocked *ranchos* left her by her father, her mother, and her three husbands.

Doña Casilda still had many years to enjoy all her wealth, since she was not quite forty. But she was not enjoying it, alone as she was and lonely, even though her many friends often came to loll through an afternoon's chocolate *merienda* among the furnishings in her living room that they never ceased to covet and admire.

Her only door and window on the Plaza belonged to this room. It ran back like a long salon, where a larger window quaffed in the light from the patio at the far end, so that the thick and uneven whitewashed walls and the coffee-hued ceiling *vigas* were neither buried in cold gloom nor lighted so much as to betray their old primitive crudeness. With a large fireplace and an ancient crucifix above it at the far corner, a rich French tapestry against the end wall, smaller oil canvases of saints in goldleaf frames along the side walls, and many polished brass candelabra standing on hand-carved chests and tables on either side, it looked to be part chapel and part drawing-room at first glance. But strewn all over the uneven floor lay thick Indian blankets, mostly a rich red, which lent so much warmth that the chapel idea gave way to that of a medieval royal drawing-room.

A queen's chamber, her friends called it, although they had never seen a queen or a castle. And, said they to themselves, it was too bad that there was no king. Only a royal consort was missing, but they went no further along this trend of thought.

Next to the front entrance a deep doorway through the thick adobe wall led to her bedroom. Her large bed by the front wall stood almost lost in shadow. Its outline and a flower-embroidered bedspread appeared faintly because a fat candle, set in a flat dish on a bracket above the bedstead, lit up a small painting of Our Lady of Light.

It was a charming miniature, finely painted over a sheet of copper, of the large central painting on the great stone reredos at the military chapel. The Lord Bishop had given it to her, the same day he consecrated the new military chapel with its wonderful reredos and the beautiful painting of Our Lady of Light enthroned in its center. Casilda was not quite seven years old then, but she remembered. No bishop from Durango had visited Santa Fe since, but she remembered how he looked and how he was dressed, because his Lordship held her on his knee and told her she was a very pretty angel. It was then that he gave her the miniature, to protect her all her life, his Lordship said, just as Mary with her Child in the painting was snatching a youth away from the jagged jaws of a fierce dragon.

And a light had burned before that little painting ever since, day and night, even after she was married—three times—when her husbands were home and also when they went away, and ever since, night and day. . . .

From the bedroom another door led into a dim dining-room, but seldom used, and from here flanking the patio followed the kitchen and other rooms, Juana's bedroom among them. Juana was an Indian girl who cooked the meals and took care of the entire house. She had been brought as a little child by Casilda's first husband when he returned from a Ute campaign, the one before the Apache battle when he was killed. Juana was a very good cook, and she took great delight in rubbing the many brass chandeliers and single candlesticks until they shone like gold. She loved Casilda like a mother and served her like a queen. Whenever they went to church, or visiting, Juana walked ahead. When going to the chapel she carried a folded blanket which she spread on the dirt floor for her mistress to kneel on during Mass, and to squat on during the sermon.

On such occasions, when not busy with the honor guard of the Palace, Captain Salazar gallantly escorted her. He was her first cousin and more like a brother, for he and Casilda had been reared together as children. He went in and out of the house as though it were his own, and no one thought evil of it because he was a good man. When soldiers say this of an officer they know well it must be true. In fact, people had thought that she should have married him, after her second husband died and she married her third. There were good reasons for the Vicar's granting a dispensation, since available younger men of her station were scarce, and she had been widowed thrice by war while he had recently lost his wife in childbirth. The captain had not married again, and it was a pity that he could not be Casilda's fourth husband.

Another but less frequent visitor was the Frenchman. He was attracted by the large store of old French and Spanish wines in a dark room off the kitchen. Her father and grandfather had for years bought the contraband Burgundy from New Orleans; the legal Spanish wines had come in casks from Jerez to Mexico City, and some bottles of it had made their way up to Santa Fe. In turn, Casilda was rewarded by the tales the Frenchman told about far Quebec and New Orleans. He had also been to Paris. Many took this foreign merchant for a spy. It was whispered about that he kept an evergrowing cache of lead ingots and kegs of gunpowder, against the day when French colonial troops from Louisiana invaded New Mexico. This gave birth to a rumor that Casilda was lending her dark storerooms to his nefarious schemes.

Captain Salazar, more than half believing the gossip, had asked Casilda if it were true, and she had angrily told him to search the entire house if he wished. Since then the Captain had not come to see her, and she had told the Frenchman to stay away.

Now she was lonelier than ever.

One cold evening in late March, Casilda sat waiting anxiously at her front window, where she often passed long hours, for the small opening provided a clear view of the treeless Plaza, where everything worthwhile knowing in Santa Fe happened, or was reported. To learn further details she sometimes sent Juana to find out. Today the new Lord Governor was to have arrived with his entourage, but the Plaza was also bare of people, save for squads of soldiers drilling in front of the Palace. Captain Salazar was setting the men through their paces.

Although her room was comfortably warm because of the droning fireplace in the far corner, Casilda shivered for the poor men in uniform out in the cold. It was so cold that none of the usual loiterers was in sight anywhere. The western sky was orange and yellow, like her fireplace behind her, and the sunset touched with flaming light the lengthy log-pillared porch of the Palace to her right and the tall adobe parapet of the military chapel opposite, to her left. But it was a cold light, frozen by the air sweeping down from the high sierra behind her house and the parish church and the eastern reaches of the town.

Besides, she missed the Captain's company.

"Juana," she called out to her girl in the kitchen. "Juana, go out and ask my cousin why the Lord Governor did not come today. And be sure to put on a blanket. The soldiers look frozen from here."

The Ute maiden went out leaning against the unseen

wind and promptly started back with Captain Salazar, who had been dismissing the guard when the servant spoke to him.

"God give you a good evening, *prima*," he said blusteringly when he came in the door, as though no angry words had ever passed between them. Making for the fireplace he turned around with his back to the flames, and began rocking in his boots to limber his toes.

"The Lord Governor and his party got bogged down at La Cienega early this afternoon. His carriage and the freight carts sank down in the mud, a runner just told me. By now the wheels ought to be gripped tight by the icy swamp."

"So there will be no reception today?"

"It would be foolish, dear cousin. Tonight his Excellency and his Lady arrive together with his staff. They are on their way from La Cienega on horseback. We will let them rest well tonight, and late tomorrow morning until the sun is well up and the air warm. Then, at ten or eleven, we escort them to the Mass of Reception at Our Lady of Light. Father Hocio thinks this plan most excellent. In the evening—you know, the ball at the Palace. May I escort you to it, Casilda?"

"Who else would? The Frenchman?" She laughed girlishly, and then invited her now thawed-out cousin to stay for supper.

The next day, from her window, Doña Casilda watched the parade from the Palace porch straight across the Plaza to the military chapel of Our Lady of Light. From early

morning the square had begun to teem with people of
every description, inhabitants of the Capital and folks from
the *ranchos* who had come in the day before, and also
many Indians from nearby Tesuque. Casilda's landowning
lady friends from town and from the country arrived
with their husbands shortly before the procession began.
It was a short one, of course, and as soon as the Lord
Governor and his retinue disappeared into the wide doorway of the military chapel, followed by the leading officials
and citizens of the region, Casilda called Juana and they
started forth in single file.

Casilda wore her best dress of black silk with a black
wool shawl over her shoulders. The smooth fair skin of
her face, and the bloom on her cheeks brought on by the
chill air, were further livened by a scarlet geranium pinned
over her black lace mantilla, just above her left temple.
Juana tended these flowers for this one use.

Captain Salazar saw them coming and ordered the guard
to attention as Casilda sauntered between the two lines of
soldiers at the church door. She bowed and smiled, and
the men grinned behind their raised muskets, which they
would not have dared do when his Excellency went by.

With Juana opening a path for her through the dark
crowded nave, Casilda pushed toward the sunlight-bathed
reredos and soon reached her accustomed place far in front
to the right, almost beneath the pulpit of carved stone.
She promptly knelt down on the blanket which her girl
had spread out on the floor.

The Lord Governor was already seated at his red-canopied throne in the transept to her left, and next to him on a chair below the platform sat his Lady. She appeared to be a very kindly woman. Casilda would find out tonight at the reception. Seated around were the Mayor and his Council, all of whom she knew well. They were all her relatives.

But standing about on either side of the throne were several strangers in the latest style of uniforms, breathtaking in their gold-braided chests and high open collars, their epaulets shimmering on wide shoulders. Their tallness and younger years obscured his Excellency in all his panoply of solid gold embroidery and bright ribbands. They were his personal staff from the City of Mexico. She tried to guess who were single and who were married, or at least widowers, when a bell in the sacristy tinkled and out came three Padres vested for a Solemn High Mass.

The celebrant was Father Hocio, the military chaplain of the Presidio and Our Lady of Light, assisted by two other Franciscans from the parish church of San Francisco up the street. Father Hocio, leaving his deacons seated by the reredos, went up the pulpit to read the royal proclamation and say some words of welcome to the Lord Governor. He did it very calmly, as if little awed by officialdom, and looked quite imposing himself, and much younger than his years, in those beautiful pearl-hued vestments. Everyone knew that he had spent long hard years in the most difficult missions, and had stared into the face of death many times as chaplain to the colonial troops. Casilda knew this well. It was he who had anointed and comforted each of her three husbands in their final hour. It was he, too, who had allayed and soothed her despairing grief, each of those three times. She trusted him with all her thoughts, and he sometimes confided in her.

If only the Crown sent new muskets to equip the militia, he had often said to her, instead of new suits for the Lord Governor's honor guard every other year, the colonial troops would not have to defend the region with fire-sharpened oakpoles for lances, and thus leave so many widows and orphans.

"Casilda, you ought to get married again," he had said to her in the sacristy, one afternoon when she had consulted him there. "You are still young and attractive, my daughter, and a lady of lineage and means. Oh, yes, I know all about that crazy superstition among your people, that no one may marry a fourth time. It is all foolishness, all plain foolishness."

New Mexico was full of males who had married three times, and there were many women who had had three husbands. In a harsh and isolated land without doctors, many a young wife died in childbirth or in one of many recurring epidemics. Surrounded as the country was by marauding Indians of every tribe, many with good firearms bought from the French along the Mississippi, scores of New Mexican husbands died in the frequent campaigns, or else were ambushed and scalped while rounding up their sheep or cattle. Usually, by the time the third marriage ended through a natural death, if not an Indian massacre, the surviving party was too old and tired to want, or attract, a fourth mating.

And so the unspoken belief had grown that a fourth marriage was either viewed askance by God or awaited with glee by mischievous evil spirits.

But Casilda had lost her men young, within the year after each marriage, all killed in a skirmish or an ambuscade. Unlike other widows, most of them poor, she had borne no children; two unborn ones had each been killed by the shocking news of violent death. This is why she always helped certain orphans in Santa Fe, but this did not fill an invisible hollow that kept on yearning for high-pitched voices and laughter among her carved chests and polished candlesticks and in her deserted patio. Perhaps this was why she never raised her voice in anger at Juana, the Ute captive whom she had reared like her own baby.

Father Hocio and his attending ministers began the Mass at the foot of the altar—after the Lord Governor had been properly welcomed and installed. Casilda set her mind at prayerful attention, as she had learned to do since she was a little girl, ever since the bishop came and blessed the new chapel and its beautiful altar, since the day her father and mother beamed with pride when his Lordship visited their house and held her on his knee, and she got that little painting of Our Lady of Light that still hung above her bed with a lit candle before it.

She did this by first contemplating the carven bas-reliefs

on the lofty stone reredos, which now loomed up mysteriously through the incense smoke that climbed up ladders of sunlight to the clerestory above.

Starting down from the rounded peak of the reredos, where the Eternal Father in his triple tiara blessed everything below, Casilda prayed for her father.

Beneath was the Madonna and Child, Our Lady of Valvanera, seated in the hollow of an ancient oak in her forest shrine in Navarre across the seas. To her she commended the saintly soul of her mother.

Below this was the panel of Santiago the Apostle, who converted Spain; he was on horseback striving with raised sword for the Spanish armies against the Moors. In panels on either side of him were San José, patron of a happy death because he died in the arms of Jesus, and San Juan Nepomuceno holding his martyr's palm. To these three she had learned with the tragic years to entrust the souls of her three martyred soldier-husbands—and strange that their names should have been Santiago, José, and Juan . . .

But to Casilda the most beautiful of all was the large oil painting of *Nuestra Señora de la Luz,* enthroned in the center of the reredos, just above the head of Father Hocio. Our Lady of Light wore a white gown and flowing blue mantle, holding her Infant on her left arm, and with the other hand rescuing a young man from the gaping maw of an infernal monster. The Holy Child smilingly directed the operation. But it seemed to Casilda that the youth being helped didn't seem to care much whether he was saved or not. The artist had given him a blank look.

Maybe he was stupid about such things, like so many people.

Anyway, the figures and colors were richly distracting. They were exactly like those in the miniature above her bed, as though that picture had been stretched out by magic to become this one on the altar, or the other way around. In fact, Casilda could do the trick at will by squinting hard . . .

By now she no longer heard Father Hocio's Latin chant, nor the shuffling and the coughing of the crowds behind her. Glancing toward the left transept, without daring to turn her head, she could plainly see a certain officer next to the Lord Governor. He was a tall Commandant, with a sharp widow's peak on his high forehead. Was he married? Such a man, surely, would not be afraid of a local superstition. From his self-assured stance, Casilda guessed, he must have been all over the world. Perhaps he was from the Court of Madrid. The thought thrilled her, for a Spaniard from Europe was a greater prize than a Creole from New Spain.

Once, for the space of a wink, Casilda was sure he had looked meaningly at her.

She would meet him at the ball tonight, and he might ask for an assignation. Still, was it not wrong to admit a stranger into one's home, and at such a late hour? What if he proposed something sinful? Officers who came to Santa Fe from the outside world were usually very bold in this regard. And Father Hocio had often preached about the dangers of becoming entangled; the near occasion of sin was more wily than the sudden bare face of evil. And yet, the Padre himself had told her that she ought to get married.

Suppose the Commandant did ask to take her home after the reception, and she declined—would he want to see her again? She was not too young any more. Under the circumstances she had a good reason to say "yes."

Sometime later, Casilda felt Juana's hand shoving something into hers under the shawl. It was a folded bit of paper. Juana whispered that she did not know who had given it to her. It must have been some other servant in the packed throng behind them. She opened the tiny sheet flat and was struck right away by the handsome script. Her full name lay traced in delicate scrolls. It was not the uneven halting handwriting of folks in Santa Fe who could write. Slowly, and with a rising thrill, she read the message:

"Not until now have I seen such a rose in full bloom, such a rare apple in full ripeness, I who have seen the best gardens and groves of the whole world. Do forgive this my heart for being overbold, my dear Lady, but it is gone mad with your beauty. May I visit with you alone tonight, after the reception at the Palace? If you accept, which you must, will you give me this sign? As you leave the chapel this morning, do not take holy water at the font. I will be watching. Kissing your hand, I am your unworthy servant and slave,

Comandante del Fuego."

Comandante del Fuego! Nobility! Perhaps the land called Tierra del Fuego was named after a great Conquistador who was his grandfather. And he himself must be the new commander of the Presidio.

It had to be the tall officer with the handsome widow's peak. Tempted to look over, she checked herself. He must surely be staring at her right now. She must give no sign of her excitement, even though she must look quite flustered already.

He looked handsomer still as he left the church with the others in the Governor's retinue. Nudging her girl, Casilda followed Juana after the crowds that were elbowing their way out into the sunlit square. Juana took holy water from the carved stone font and crossed herself as she went out the door. Casilda reached out by force of habit, paused for a moment, and then brought her hand back under the shawl on her arm, where she still held the folded bit of paper in a trembling clenched fist.

It was like a dream, the way she and Juana skirted around the rear of the milling throngs on the Plaza, still cheering the Lord Governor as he vanished into the Palace. They reached home unnoticed, and Casilda began ordering the girl to sweep and dust the entire house and polish the brass candelabra, although she had done all this yesterday.

The evening arrived in a hurry. Shortly before eight, Casilda received word from Captain Salazar that he could not come for her. So much the better, she thought.

When the time came, Juana led her across the short

corner-space of Plaza to the main entrance of the Palace of the Governors. The long parapet of its *portal,* and the whole Plaza in front, were already powdered white with the first flakes of a snowfall that promised to flutter down all night. While she loved snow, to watch through the window from her cozy room, tonight she enjoyed walking on it. It reminded her of clouds, and her feet treading on them far above the real world.

As Juana hied herself to the servants' quarters beyond the wide *zaguán,* Casilda went into the Palace ballroom to make her own grand entrance. Some of her friends and relations came forward to greet her and then presented her to the Lord Governor and his Lady. Her Ladyship at close range proved to be what she had appeared in church. But soon Casilda was away with the new officers, all most charming in their manner and address. All of them took turns in dancing with her whenever the musicians struck up a *seguidilla.*

But none of them was named "del Fuego." And she dared not ask. Perhaps one of these strangers had played a prank on her to amuse his companions, for these court people from the Viceregal Capital of New Spain felt themselves much superior to the best in the provinces. She must not give them the chance of enjoying the success of their prank.

She also looked in vain for Captain Salazar. He must have been called away on something really important and serious, to miss this reception even when he had been unable to escort her to it. Harried by her suspicions, Casilda excused herself well before midnight and joined her girl in the hallway, where Juana had been waiting for some time.

Outside, the snow had risen to the height of a man's hand, and the swirling flakes were coming down thicker than before. As Juana plunged ahead into the white world, the strong hand of a man reached out from the shadows of the *portal* and took Casilda's shoulder. She turned to see a tall military figure in a great dark cape half-hidden by the black shade of a wooden pillar. But there was enough light from a window to bring out his handsome features at the moment, and a bit of the widow's peak.

"I am the Comandante del Fuego," he said. "I could not come to the ball because one of my men shot himself tonight, and I could not leave him until—Casilda, may I still come?"

"But of course," she stammered quickly.

He was indeed far more handsome, and taller, than the other staff officers she had danced with tonight, Casilda thought breathlessly as she caught up silently behind Juana, who had not felt her absence for the moment. And how tender and considerate the Commandant must be, if he missed the reception to stay by the side of a common soldier in his last need.

After she had revived the flames in the corner fireplace, and brought out two bottles of the Burgundy and the Jerez, which the Frenchman said were of the best, she touched a long sliver of pine to the fire and glided with it from candle to candle all around the room until it glittered like a palace in dreams.

She had barely fastened the shutters of her window when a soft knock at the door made her reach it quickly to pull back the bolt. Hastily shaking the snow off his mantle, and off his pointed admiralty hat that had an ostrich plume running fore and aft, the Commandant stepped in and stood for a second smiling down. The splendor of his thickly gallooned scarlet uniform, the height and width of the epauleted shoulders, the masterful long head from the wonderful widow's peak on the brow down to the firm manly chin, all of it held her fast and breathless.

He then looked about the room, scowled a trifle at the pictures on the walls, and then with long strides went about blowing out all the candles until only two were left burning on the wine table toward the front.

"The room is magnificent," he said, breathing deeply from his effort, and offering excuses for his sudden behavior. "The place was much too brilliant, and it is you I came to see, my dear lady."

"How gallant you are, my Commandant, in everything," she replied, still breathless. "There are no such men here in Santa Fe. It is like the ways of the French Court."

"But of course, of course, my dear Casilda. For it is I who taught the French Court its ways!"

He chuckled heartily, very much pleased by this retort, and she no less than enchanted by it. Banter like this, and more, melted any reserve or misgivings she might have had. He deftly opened both bottles and poured the wine into the waiting glasses. When she told him when and how it had reached Santa Fe, he began painting before her wide-open eyes the beauties of far-away France and Spain in a way that made the Frenchman's talk sound like boorish nonsense. While describing the boudoir of Marie Antoinette at Versailles, he casually looked over her shoulder toward her bedroom's doorway and suggested that she show him the rest of the house. And as though she were obeying a command, Casilda stood up and moved into the next room, he very close to her, his long arm across her shoulders.

His fingers twitched once, very lightly, and overwhelming memories of many years past surged up within her like a fever.

Her companion jerked to a stop and took in his breath sharply. They were standing just inside the bedroom. She looked up to find him eyeing the figures in the little candlelit painting above her bed. She could hear something like a growl, as an unfriendly dog growls, deep inside of him, when he muttered gruffly:

"Put out that light."

"No," she answered promptly, without thinking. "No!"

"Put out that light, I tell you!" His voice was a roar.

Casilda's heart quivered. Her limbs felt cold and weak. For the face above her was changing. As it glared down at her she saw that the handsome widow's peak looked hackly and mangy, like an angry cat's fur. What were pale blue eyes before were now a cat's sulphury yellow. One searing iris bore straight down into her, the other was turned out of balance, but she felt it also looking at her. His big smile was now a leer, drooling over the outstretched lower lip, and the large teeth were not white and even, but yellow and set apart from each other.

Satan could not look worse.

"*Jesús! María!*" she shrieked.

A flashing explosion threw her to the floor. Blinded for a second, but not knocked out of her senses, she felt some new strength in her that kept her from swooning, even though she found herself flat on the floor. From where she lay she saw eerie streaks of ill-smelling fumes streaming out into her living room and out through the open front door. A cold river of air was flowing in under that of the escaping smoke.

When at last she rose up to close the door, she could not help glancing toward the deserted Plaza. It was all white, perfectly white in the moonlight.

But leading from her threshold into what seemed infinity was a line of black marks—not of footsteps, but of cloven hooves.

Just then Captain Salazar rushed in from the side, from the direction of his quarters.

"Casilda, what happened?" he cried, grasping her shoulders. "I heard a big noise as I was coming home to bed. What happened?"

"Nothing happened, my Captain," she replied, hoping he would not see the marks on the snow. "I fainted and fell down, one of those things you men know nothing about. And I came to breathe some fresh air. That is all."

But he was already sniffing suspiciously inside the house. "Gunpowder. I smell gunpowder, Casilda, and I did hear an explosion. Dear cousin, I am going to search this house tomorrow!"

She smiled straight at him. His comical suspicion helped so much. "Dear cousin of mine, you smell what you wish to smell and hear what you wish to hear."

But this relief was not enough for her. To hide a fearful trembling that she felt returning, she asked the Captain why he had not gone to the reception.

"Oh, that," he said. "Shortly before eight a drunken soldier shot himself in the head. You know the man, *El Períco*, that vagrant from Guatemala who joined the Presidio last year. A worse foul-mouthed blasphemer I had never seen in all my life. A son of the devil he was. For almost four hours Father Hocio tried to get him to repent, but to his last breath he cursed us all and the Padre. So I could not escort you to the ball, dear cousin. Well, it is time to go, and here is Juana to assist you. God give you both a good night, and we shall see tomorrow about the gunpowder."

With this, Captain Salazar strode out the door. Casilda was vastly relieved to see that some merciful gusts of wind had meanwhile erased the trail of hooves outside. But the meaning of her sinister visitor's name and title, "Commander of the Fire," brought on such a horrible trembling once more that Juana had to assist her into bed, and also crawl in with her for the rest of the night.

THE BLACK EWE

AFTER PENNING UP THE BLACK EWE IN THE SMALL round palisade of juniper posts behind the low adobe house, old Agapito stacked some hay against the palings; then he filled the hewn-log trough with water from the stream close by. This ewe, which he had raised from a lamb, was most unlike the gray and brownish flocks. The fine wool alone, and the almost jet sheen of it, set her off from thousands of others.

The *patrón* had entrusted this sheep to his care all winter, but now he had ordered Agapito to leave her in the corral at San Blas, so that he might enjoy the sight of her,

he said. When the master used the female pronoun, however, Agapito could not help thinking of something else.

San Blas was but a handful of earthen huts by the shallow Rio Puerco where the wives of the sheepherders stayed while their men went out on the range with the flocks shared out to each one. Young or old, most of these women had families to keep them busy day and night; a certain young one, however, had become a byword among the herders when her husband was beyond earshot.

Although the hacienda of the *patrón* was on the great river in the valley, north of the Indian pueblo of Isleta, the master often came to San Blas and stayed a few days each time to oversee the work, so he said; for he seldom went out to the pastures where the sheep were grazing. This time he had called for Agapito and the black ewe, telling him to leave her with him in San Blas. But now, as the old herder was about to leave with his sheep for his own range of pastureland, he did not look into the master's eye. Gravely doffing his tattered sombrero, Agapito bowed deeply and trudged off under the hot afternoon sun with a heavy heart.

Not that Agapito had any worries of his own, or about his own, for he had no kin. He was a gaunt gentle fellow with the white beard of a Spanish grandee set on a kindly Indian-like face, and this made it look almost false. Standing among his sheep he looked from afar like a scarecrow in a cottonfield. Nobody remembered where he had come from, for he had not been born in the region. He was by far the best sheepherder on the *patrón's* vast *rancho*, venturing alone deep into the Navajo country where virgin pastures lay, since these wild people did not have many sheep or horses in those days. It was told about that the Navajos never bothered him or his flocks when other herders closer to the valley had to be ever on the watch against a raid.

Nor did his fellow sheepherders envy him in the least, but rather sought his advice about the care of sheep, even if they let his counsels go unheeded whenever idleness or thievery could be covered up by blaming coyotes, the weather, or the Navajos. It was to him that they came in time of sickness, whether it was a lamb or one of their own children. For Agapito held the secret of various herbs, and his hands, they said, had the touch of prayer.

The *patrón*, still handsome and vigorous despite his graying hairs, took it for granted that the flocks Agapito cared for were the fattest and the most fruitful, as they had always been since he could remember, for the old fellow had served his father quite as faithfully. And he did treat him with all due kindness, after his own reserved fashion, just as he now, for example, showed a quiet tender concern for the black ewe.

But to the *patrón's* wife, who always stayed at the hacienda by the river, Agapito was not merely a sheepherder but a shepherd, clothed with the aura which this word has kept from the gospels and the psalms.

As Agapito followed his close-packed bleating sheep eager to reach their usual feeding grounds, he was thinking of Doña Eduvíges down at the hacienda and felt very sorry for her. A true lamb of the Lord's flock she was, he thought to himself—yes, a white ewe. He was not startled by this comparison that came to his head; his mind could not have formed a more flattering likeness for someone so meek and good. Although her grandparents had been great captains in the conquest of the land, she did not look down on her household servants but regarded them more like cousins. Agapito felt like the father that he never was as she embraced him whenever he came to the hacienda. And though she was past middle age, her dainty hands and her clear blue eyes, the grace she lent to her sweeping skirt and slender bodice, all presented something beautiful to be worshipped.

He would never forget that time when the rattlesnake bit him. While cutting across a field towards the rambling hacienda under the great cottonwoods, he had stepped on what his aging eyes told him was a long-dried cow dropping; the angered coiled viper dug viciously into his foot through the torn rough-hide shoe. As soon as he reached the house, Doña Eduvíges tore off the shoe, and slashing the flesh with a razor over the ugly marks of the fangs, began sucking and spitting out the dark gory ooze until she was satisfied that the color of the blood was as it should be.

It was like the story he had many times heard of her namesake, that great noble lady of bygone days, Saint Hedwigis, washing and kissing the sores on the feet of lepers. This thought did not disturb Agapito in the least, for no one knew better than he that sheepherders' feet are not very clean things. Afterwards, having washed both his feet and bandaged the injured one with cool linen strips over the herbs he took out of his pack, she had put him to bed, in the great white bed where she and the *patrón* slept —for he was at San Blas at the time—and there she kept him for some days until the fever that had set in was finally gone.

All that time, however, he had watched the deep sadness in her blue eyes, and he knew that she knew without saying a word. Indeed, her eyes seemed to say that he also knew and ought to do something about it. But how can a poor *peón* give counsels in such matters to his *patrón*?

It was drawing on to dusk and Agapito was still far away from his usual range, having traveled but a few hours from San Blas. First he drove his sheep into the shelter of a blind canyon, low and shallow, which he had often used before. At its mouth he sat down to munch a piece of dry bread and some jerked meat, then prepared his bed on the soft sand that had drifted into a shallow cave under the low sandstone cliff. But try as he would, he could not fall asleep. The thought of the master at San Blas plagued him like a dull toothache. If he could not admonish the *patrón*, and much less stop his coming to San Blas, he could at least pray for his sake, and Doña Eduvíges' especially.

How long he prayed he did not know, except that the full moon, after coming up like an overripe squash above the far valley where the hacienda lay, rose steadily higher and smaller into the velvet night, its light sharper and more silvery as it dwindled in size. The sharpening moonlight had backed up over the canyon floor, like the imperceptible rise of a flood, until it crept along the outer edge of the little cave.

It was then that Agapito, for all his years, sat bolt upright. Someone was crossing the sandy bottom and coming up the small slope toward his shelter. It was a lone Indian, a tall Navajo.

He had never seen a Navajo so tall. He threw a shadow like that of a long pine tree. He was naked except for a breechclout, as Navajos went about in those times. His chest and limbs, even his cheeks, were streaked with weird jagged lines, luminous in the moonlight. Whether warrior on the warpath or medicineman on a cure, or both, he carried a war club and some scalps on his belt, as also some trinkets of human bone dangling from it. But all this did not amaze Agapito so much as the fact that the warrior or witch doctor was carrying a sheep, a black sheep, across his broad shoulders.

It was the *patrón's* black ewe. There was no other one like it in the whole country; and if there were, Agapito could have picked it out from a whole flock of black ewes.

First, Agapito uttered a greeting in Navajo, for he knew a few phrases of the language. The Indian grunted a courteous but curt reply, and then continued in Spanish, a very smooth Spanish. No Navajo knew more than a few Spanish words, but this witch doctor spoke the language better than Agapito himself, better even than the *patrón* and Doña Eduvíges. His inflections were more like those of the Lord Governor himself, who had stopped at the hacienda with his retinue once when Agapito happened to be there overnight.

Still, this did not keep the old man's eyes from wandering away from the black ewe, which trembled and struggled in stark terror. However, the Indian's two giant fists gripped each pair of legs like a scabbard around a rusted sword. And yet, all this was not half so outlandish as the request the visitor was making in very high Castilian. It was more of a command.

"Agapito, the master wishes you to shear the black ewe tonight, right away. I shall hold it for you and, after you

have shorn off the fleece—closely and evenly, mind you!—
I shall return both sheep and wool to the master."

His eyes lit up sharply and seemed to spit forth fire
when Agapito did not offer to make a move.

"Simpleton!" he hissed fiercely. "Get up before I make
you. Here, take these freshly ground shears which I brought
along."

The old fellow obeyed as though in a trance. His
thoughts moved about freely, however, knocking against
each other like panicky wild horses shut inside a small
oval corral after a roundup. As he began to clip off the
wool while the Indian's massive arms pinned the ewe
to the sandy ground, he wondered what this *cacique* was
doing all alone in San Blas, and so close to the valley. If
he had stolen the black ewe as the prized prey that it was,
why did he want it shorn now when the wool was not yet
full-grown? But there was no answer to these jumbled
questions. The stampede in his mind merely served to
raise greater clouds of dust.

Nor could he understand why the ewe bleated and
struggled so much. It was not the way of sheep; her
alarmed cries were more like those of a frightened nanny-
goat. What with the poor light of the moon and the
animal's spasmodic struggles, not to mention his own
poor eyesight and the whirl in his brain, Agapito pinched
and cut the pulsating hide several times. The master
would be very much displeased.

At last the distasteful task was over. As the shearer got
up and stepped back, the Indian's arms and fingers re-

laxed somewhat. In that instant the ewe broke loose and scampered madly down the silvery sandbed. Promptly, and very gracefully, the Navajo unslung his war club and sent it speeding like a hawk after a low-flying grouse. The heavy stone end caught the ewe in the middle of the back, and she rolled over with a heart-rending cry, like the pained shriek of a woman in the still of night.

The Indian ran down to it, stuck the club back in his belt, slung the limp animal across his neck—all this in one flowing movement—and kept on running like an unburdened antelope in the direction of San Blas. Agapito cupped his gnarled hands and shouted for him to come back for the wool, but the Navajo kept on bounding across the rise and fall of the moonlit landscape, when suddenly a black cloud blanketed the moon, throwing the whole countryside and the enchanted sheepherder into total darkness.

Agapito did not even lie down to sleep. Early at dawn, before the sun slipped out of the horizon where he had watched the moon come up the night before, he was driving his bleating herd back over the yellowish rolling grasslands toward San Blas. In his knapsack rode the balls of black wool which the Indian had left in his haste. If he had any misgivings, they were too vague to chase away the prayers he kept telling on the beads around his neck. But why a dumb animal should be the one to suffer, this bothered him. He would look into the corral as soon as he arrived.

By midmorning he came within sight of San Blas and of the low adobe dwelling where the master was staying. Behind it lay the corral along the little stream. But there was the *patrón* already, and running forward to meet him, an unusual thing for a *patrón* to do, as if he had been watching anxiously and eagerly for his appearance all morning.

"Come into the house right away, old man, my friend," he said, his handsome face drawn so tightly down as to show the red flesh under his lower eyelids.

"Agapito, something terrible happened to *her* last night!"

Without a word, Agapito unslung his pack and laid it by the door, then stepped inside, his master respectfully holding the door for him and following after. In a corner was a bed, which was a large bison hide stretched across a square frame slung from the ceiling *vigas* by four stout braided thongs. On it lay a moaning young woman covered with a blanket. Her head was wrapped in a towel which she held with both hands.

Her eyes stared with terror from the frame made by her forearms and elbows.

"It is her back," said the *patrón*. "As though it were broken. But she does not remember falling out of bed. I myself did not hear her fall." Here he stopped short, like a child waiting for a scolding, or worse.

Agapito set to work. The woman moaned and shrieked when he and the master slowly turned her face-downward.

Modestly, Agapito raised her blouse a little and lowered her skirt a bit at the small of her back. In doing so his deft fingers found the spinal bone that was out of place.

He ordered her to say the Apostles' Creed. It was commonly used as a measure of time in those days, but she also took it as part and parcel of the old sheepherder's curing powers. In a way it was, for, as she was engrossed in reciting the articles of faith correctly, Agapito suddenly pressed heavily with both thumbs and jerked the bone back into place.

The swinging lariat thongs sang out and were drowned at once by the woman's piercing cry of pain and surprise. The towel fell from her head, revealing a close-clipped scalp which was chafed and bruised in several spots. She looked so utterly funny that Agapito might have laughed, had he been a laughing man, or if much more serious thoughts were not beginning to make sense in his muddled head.

Reaching down for the towel she wrapped it around her bare pate in a fluster of deepest shame. The hair on a woman's head is her crowning glory—now they knew what it meant, Agapito and the *patrón*, too. With her thick black tresses this now pitiable creature had been quite a beautiful woman, even to Agapito's disinterested eye. For he had known her since she was born, the child of a Pawnee squaw captured on the bison plains and of the Spanish soldier who had brought her in. Many of these *genízaras* were often prettier and more appealing than the Spanish women.

Muttering something about herbs, Agapito went out to his knapsack by the door. By now he was not surprised to find two long braids and the rest of a woman's hair instead of the much bulkier balls of black wool. Taking out a leather pouch filled with herbs he returned to the room and began making a paste from various dried leaves and roots. This he applied as a poultice on the woman's sore back, and even persuaded her to let him use it as a salve on her ravaged head.

Then the master followed the servant to the round corral at the rear of the house.

There, peacefully browsing, as innocent as any young sheep can be, no matter what the hue of her coat, was the black ewe with all her wool. As both men watched the glint of sun outlining her slow movements with gold, Agapito began to tell his story. When he was finished he looked at the *patrón* straight in the eye.

Doña Eduvíges became a very happy lady although she never heard about what happened at San Blas. The village is no more because this took place a couple of centuries ago, before long periods of drought turned the grasslands into a desert, when the sheepherders abandoned their homes there, and the once shallow Rio Puerco cut through the site to form the wide and deep black arroyo that you see today.

WAKE
FOR DON CORSINIO

THE SUDDEN NIGHT OF THE PLAINS HAD DRAPED A
black pall over the prairie-clay houses of El Piojo. But
away from the small plaza, on a faint slope to the east, a
big bonfire fiercely lit up the flat-roofed ranch house of
Don Felipe. The duller light of kerosene lamps shone
dead through the front windows and open doorways. A
slight but steady nightwind carried the shrill cries of small
boys romping around the fire, and sometimes the murmur
of gruffer voices praying in unison inside the house.

Once in a while an *alabado*, yelled out dolefully from a
strong male voice, came out and boarded the nightwind.

This was answered sometimes by the woeful call of a coyote out on the prairie, and once the answer came in the faint trailing moan of a locomotive from the direction of Las Vegas much further away.

It seemed as though nature as well as man, including his latest invention which had lately spun its threads of steel across San Miguel County, were all mourning the untimely passing of Don Corsinio. *Pobrecito*, everyone was saying or thinking—poor little man.

They had found him late in the afternoon after a brief but furious thunderstorm, about a mile away from El

Piojo. The cold rain had soaked him to the skin, and parts of his clothes were burned off, also a sizable circle of buffalo grass around him. Nearby lay an empty smudged jug.

First the lightning must have struck him and set him afire, and then the same thunderhead belatedly took pity on him and put out the flames with a nozzle-burst of rain. This had served to chill him to death if the lightning bolt had not fully sheared away his life beforehand. Most likely he had felt no pain, for he was very drunk early that afternoon when someone saw him reeling slowly out to the prairie, jug in hand—to round up his cattle, he had said.

Poor little man. He had no cattle. He had lost all his big herds since he became a daily customer at the saloon, another institution that came with the railroad to Las Vegas and spawned little offshoots in scattered villages like El Piojo. Since the day his lovely wife Barbara died, Don Corsinio had not only lost himself in drink but all of his earthly goods as well. Not that he had squandered it all on liquor. Somehow, his branded steers and cows had vanished from the common grazing land on the plains, and his horses, too, and his hogs and chickens from his corrals, not to mention his harnesses and tools from the sheds.

One by one the handsome furnishings which had been Barbara's pride and joy had also disappeared from the house—even a large square board with a picture of Santa Barbara painted on it.

This painting Don Corsinio himself had bartered for a

week's ration from the bartender, whose wife had long coveted it.

This same woman now sat with her neighbors around the corpse, and was thinking of St. Barbara as the heavenly protector against lightning. The saintly virgin's pagan father was struck dead by a bolt from heaven after he cut off his daughter's head for being a Christian. First he had kept her locked up in a castle tower, which explained the look of her crown, like a parapet. The sword in her hand told the story of her death.

And now Don Corsinio had died like that heathen. Was he so punished for getting rid of her picture so cold-heartedly, in exchange for a jug of whisky? Anyway, Santa Barbara had come into better hands which appreciated her much more than this poor drunken fool. May he rest in peace, the woman prayed with the other mourners. Poor little man.

Don Felipe, who had offered his own house for the wake and his foodstuffs for the all-night feeding of the guests, sat quietly in one corner of the room. He also gave the dead man his own black Sunday suit and laid him out on his sheet-covered table, after shaving him with his own hands and razor. For Corsinio and Felipe had known each other since they were boys back at San Miguel del Vado, long before they got large grants on the eastern plain and moved out with their wives and other families to found El Piojo.

How different Corsinio was then, young and fine-look-

ing, and always happy. It was he who had unwittingly
named the new place, when he said that the little brown
settlement on the bare prairie looked like a louse on the
earth's bald head. Everyone had prospered on the new
land, but none like Corsinio, who had the most uncanny
luck with livestock. Some said it was because he and pretty
Barbara loved each other so much.

But some lesser folks envied them and were well-primed
to take advantage of Corsinio from the moment he let
drink ruin him after Barbara died. Not so his boyhood
friend Don Felipe, who had tried every means to save
him, and his belongings also. But to no avail. Now he had
done his final best for his friend, aged and dead long before his time. The shaven face and the neat black suit, and
the warm candles around the corpse, made him look
more like the handsome Corsinio of former days. But it
was too late now. Poor little man.

Don Felipe was startled from his reverie by the *alabado*
man's bursting into a screaming dirge that made the
candles in the close room ward off the blow with little
elbows of flame. The fellow's scrawny horseface whinnied
with such soulful grief that Don Felipe could not help
thinking about Corsinio's cattle and horses. For the singer
was at the head of the lot which had rustled all the livestock piecemeal, and peddled them at the railroad stock-
yards in Las Vegas. They now sat all around the room
with such doleful looks, beside their conniving sallow
wives who had ransacked poor Barbara's home after her

death, all joining in the chorus as if their very hearts would break.

More than once Don Felipe had complained to the sheriff and others in town, but in vain, for the singer controlled most of the votes in El Piojo as head of the secret society that did bloody penances every Holy Week. And now their chants and prayers. As if all this made up for what they had done. Don Felipe wondered what sort of warped minds these *genízaros* had.

For the families of Corsinio and Felipe, and a couple of others, were the only ones that could be called Spanish. The rest were a mixture of Plains Indians tribes, whose forebears had been captured in battle and reared in Spanish families. The singer's own parents had been a French-Canadian vagrant and his Shoshone squaw who had drifted down from Taos to San Miguel long ago. The parents and grandparents of these people had become Mexican citizens when the New World broke away from Spain, and now their children were American voters. Not all were bad by any means, but even the best were a bundle of superstitions, ancient tribal fears remembered and grafted onto Spanish Christian customs.

Unlike Felipe, Corsinio had never harbored any ill-will or disdain for these creatures, yet, see what they had done to him. *Pobrecito.*

Poor little man! Had someone ever told Don Corsinio the stir he would cause in the lives of El Piojo, he would have laughed himself to death. But now he was dead anyhow, or so his mourners thought. One of them fancied he saw an arm move slightly, and was blaming a shadow cast by the candles, when the corpse did sit up on the table of a sudden, not with a quick start, yet fast enough to charge the room with terror.

With horrified screams the men and women nearest the door scrambled madly out into the night. Those along the rear wall rushed through the adjoining kitchen, stampeding cooks and helpers before them, as well as the children playing outside. The dying bonfires sent up sprays of sparks high into the black sky when people ran through them in their eagerness to get away, and all kept running in one drove down the slope until they reached their huddled houses in the village. Bolting their doors behind them, they lit all the lamps and candles they could find and knelt down on the earthen floors to pray for the rest of the night, some women and children keeping on their wailing for hours after.

Poor Don Corsinio. For a good while he did not know where he was, sitting there on the white-sheeted table and rubbing his eyes and cheeks, then his arms and legs. But the warmth of the now jolly dipping candles felt good, although at first he did not know what caused the comfortable glow around him. As he rubbed his cleanshaven face further, and then noticed the black suit he was wearing, the white table and candles (and their meaning) began to come into focus. He called out but there was no answer. Again he called out, and this time he pronounced a name.

"Barbara!"

"Here I am, my dear Corsinio."

Through the bedroom door opposite she came toward him, repeating his name most tenderly. It was his wife, as fresh and as lovely as the first year they were married.

But why was she wearing a golden crown, shaped like the parapet of a castle tower? And why the sword in her hand? Unless it was not his wife, really, but Santa Barbara, just as she looked on that painting which he had traded for whisky.

And yet, her face and smile were those of Barbara his wife. Even her figure was his own Barbara's, when she was big with child shortly before she died. And still, he recalled, this was also the shape of the saint on the *retablo*. The Chimayó man who had painted it long ago knew nothing of perspective and, in copying the wide flounce of the martyred virgin's regal skirt, he had made her appear what she most certainly was not in this respect.

But her voice, it was his wife's voice without a doubt. Santa Barbara or plain Barbara, he must have arrived in heaven or the borders thereof. For his good wife must have gone to heaven, surely. What disturbed him now was the fact that he himself should be there.

"You are not dead," Barbara was saying, with that smile he remembered so well. "Do you not remember this afternoon, when you went out to round up your cows, the cows that are no longer there? There was a great thundercloud overhead."

"And I was struck by lightning."

"No, no, Corsinio, it was not that. You could no longer stand up, and so you sat down on the buffalo grass. Then you decided to roll a cigarette and smoke it. This is when you fainted and the dry grass caught on fire."

"And I was burned to death?"

"No, no, Corsinio." (How well he remembered her tone of sweet forebearance when she used to say "no" twice before his name.) "My dear husband, the cloudburst put out the fire on the ground and on your clothes. But it left you so cold and stiff that the people believed you were really dead, struck dead by lightning."

"So the thundercloud saved me," Corsinio began to muse. "The great Santa Barbara, the patron of thunder and lightning—she came and saved my life. And you also, Barbara, my wife . . ."

He covered his face with both hands as if to keep a rise of sobs from shaking his head loose. For now a bitter memory came back to him, one that had lain hidden deep inside these past few years. Maybe it was the sword in her hand that brought it back.

In those happy days he had a sword like it, and which he prized the way a child does a toy. It had belonged to his grandfather as first commander of the old Spanish fort of San Miguel on the Pecos. One day he could not find it and he accused Barbara of hiding it or giving it away, for he knew that she abhorred the sight of swords and big knives. When she denied it he slapped her.

Only once he slapped her, on the cheek. It was the first and last time he ever struck Barbara, in fact, the only time he was ever angry at her. Right away he knelt down to beg her forgiveness; and she forgave him, right away.

Some days after, the baby was born, dead. And then Barbara died.

"A mere slap on the cheek never hurt anyone, except their feelings, and mine were not hurt," Barbara was saying, as she took his hands away from his face and held them in hers.

The sword was no longer in sight, but Corsinio marveled less at this than at the way she was reading his thoughts.

"You foolish boy, that slap had nothing to do with the baby's death and mine. We were to leave you anyway. Now you will never get drunk any more, Corsinio."

It was like a bright light, this revelation, which for the moment rubbed out the sputtering candles alongside and the lamps on the walls. At the same time his stomach winced and his whole frame shuddered at the very mention of his getting drunk. Barbara laughed and told him that he looked hungrier than a coyote, the same words she used whenever he came home from work on the range. After removing the candles, she helped him off the table to his feet and led him into the kitchen where the *velorio* supper lay untouched. Helping him to a bench, she poured him some coffee and raised the cup to his lips. The first swallow made him feel steadier, in his head as well as his limbs. The set table before him, the entire room, began to appear more solid and real as he slowly ate the morsels of red *chile* and chopped meat that she kept putting in his mouth.

"You must go away from El Piojo forever, Corsinio," she was saying over his shoulder. "Go back to San Miguel, and get yourself another good woman to be your help and companion."

Corsinio turned around to reply, but she was no longer behind him or anywhere in the kitchen. Hearing footsteps in the mourning room he went in to speak to her, but ran into Don Felipe instead. Both men looked at each other in bewilderment for some moments, then embraced each other firmly and solemnly.

Don Felipe had been swept ahead by the frightened human wave when dead Don Corsinio suddenly came to life. Not that he would have stood calmly by, but he would have collected his wits about him instead of rushing pell-mell with the herd down to the village. There he found himself locked inside the bartender's home, together with this man's family and his own wife and children. These people were Spanish also, and close friends of the family, so that their coming together was no mystery.

But like their more ignorant neighbors, their hosts began lighting up every candle in the house and placing them before the painting of Santa Barbara. The lady of the house was swearing solemnly to the saint that she would be returned to Don Corsinio's house the first thing in the morning.

This gave Don Felipe some very practical ideas. Ignoring the pleas of his family and hosts, he came back to his ranch house to find his old friend walking about—in fact, the corpse partaking of the wake's refreshments. Corsinio was beginning to enjoy this, but soon grew serious and began telling all about Barbara, the dead wife and the martyr-saint, or both combined, and what they had said. Don Felipe nodded understandingly, and he also noted the sweat-beads of fever breaking out on the sick man's brow.

"This is all very good, Corsinio," he spoke at last, when the feverish man had exhausted himself talking. "But let us keep it a big secret, all that Barbara told you. Let the people keep on thinking that you really came back from the dead, and I will spread the word around that you know who robbed you. When you go back to San Miguel you will have most of your possessions back."

For some days Don Corsinio actually lay at death's door with pneumonia, carefully tended by Don Felipe and his wife, who found no difficulty in keeping visitors away. When he finally regained his strength, weeks later, the unkempt poor little man had vanished. It was the young-looking Corsinio, if somewhat haggard and less bouncy, who went home one day to find all the rooms furnished as in former times.

Santa Barbara hung from the same nail, with her castle-like coronet and sword, and her queerly shaped skirt. There was a box on the table heaped with silver dollars, the price of many cattle, horses, and hogs. In the barn was a team of horses, their complete harness hanging neatly along the walls, and his own wagon.

The following day he put everything in the wagon and started out for San Miguel, Santa Barbara perched on the high seat beside him.

THE LEAN YEARS

SAN JOSÉ WAS THE PATRON SAINT OF LA CUNITA, and the priest of Las Vegas gladly braved the prairie March winds each year to be at the fiesta. He loved the little town's setting, cradled as it was in a little hollow where the barish foothills of the great sierras came down to meet the plains. Beyond the double row of adobe houses and the chapel was a delightful small canyon with a dwarf forest of pines and scruboaks. But even this was not enough reward for a long journey on horseback in mid-March.

Perhaps it was the people themselves, some twenty families of simple folks who sat wide-eyed in the chapel lis-

tening to him tell about San José, and how his tall flowering staff was a symbol of his chaste and loving care for the Virgin Mother and her Divine Child.

It was the same sermon year after year, but, like children, they listened to it each year as though it were for the first time. Especially young José Vera, who sat in the front bench while the other male villagers followed an unpleasant custom of crowding near the door. If not gazing intently at the preacher, José's eyes rested on the saint's statue above the altar.

An ugly monster it was, this image, if only three feet

tall, the Padre could not help thinking. It shocked his
French sensibilities with its stiff poise, its cheap tin coronet, its staring almond eyes on a narrow yellowish face,
and, worst of all, the unreal black beard that was nothing
more than a patch of black paint smeared around the thin
drab lips. It shocked the sugary false baroque ideals in
which he had been reared. And still, he was human enough
to imagine that the people themselves did see there a
beauty beyond his ken, like the mother of the ugliest brat
who thinks he has the face of an angel. The image that
love forms in her eyes and heart is real, and so was theirs,
he reasoned. They saw, perhaps more clearly than he himself could, the true *chevalier* features of Joseph of Nazareth,
a poor carpenter but also a veritable gentleman of the royal
house of David.

After the Mass José Vera came to the sacristy, as he always did, and kissed the Padre's hand. His ecstasy during
the sermon still glowed on his plain, kindly face.

"Padre, it was a most beautiful fiesta this year. It gets
better every year. Especially your sermon about San José,
it was very beautiful. And did you notice the new paper
flowers on the saint's staff? And the new purple dress?
They are beautiful."

Yes, he had not failed to notice that sickening mauve
of the gown which common folks call purple. It rendered
the lemon countenance more sulphurous. Catching himself scowling, the priest smiled benignly down at José.

"It was all most magnificent, José, and so I thanked the
people for the new mud plaster all around the chapel,

and for the clean white walls inside. The fine purple dress of San José, a little too short maybe, is also magnificent."

José beamed with pride, and the priest braced himself to listen with forebearance to what the youth was beginning to say. He had heard the story many times. But if José enjoyed the same sermon year after year, it was nothing but right that he himself showed some interest when the tables, or rather the pulpit, were turned around.

"My father built this chapel, years before I was born, when La Cunita was new. He also helped build all of the houses. You see, his name was also José Vera and he was a carpenter like San José, as I myself am also a carpenter and my name is José Vera. My father also made the altar, but he did not carve and paint the shells and the flowers on it. Nor did he make the image of San José. There were no *santeros* among the people who first came here to La Cunita with my father from the Rio Grande across the sierras. So they hired a man who knew how to carve and paint *santos* to come from Las Trampas. Then he went back.

"But my father and the other people, they stayed. He married my mother, and then I was born and was called José like San José and my father. My mother died when I was little and they buried her in the *campo santo,* over near the front door of the chapel. I grew up and my father taught me to be a carpenter like himself and San José. Then he died, and they buried him by my mother."

The Padre found an opening. "And now, José, it is your turn to get married, like your father. I saw Soledad looking at you from the corner of her eye during the sermon. She is a pretty girl."

The young man blushed and bowed his black head slightly. "If she will have me, I will gladly marry her."

He had no need to feel so backward, the priest thought. His regular features were pleasing and his limbs well-fashioned from hard work. He was by far the best pick in all the village for a good girl like Soledad. Surely, a word from himself to Soledad and her parents before he returned to Las Vegas would make the path smooth for the boy.

José grinned. "Thank you very much, *señor*. If Soledad will have me, I will care for her the way San José looked after blessed Mary and her little Jesus."

Then he paused and squinted at the priest, a deep problem carved on the wrinkles above his nose.

"What is it, José?"

"Padre, in your sermon this year you said something new at the end, about another Joseph who provided for all his people. And there were seven lean years and seven years of plenty. I—I did not understand."

Neither did the other townsfolk. The priest was sorry from the very moment he introduced the new idea, when he saw a thin fog of bewilderment float before their fixed gaze. Involved allegories were too much for ordinary folks, and most likely this one had fled their minds by now—except José's. José did have to remember. Now it was his duty to explain it further with all patience.

"It goes this way, my son. Joseph of Egypt, who lived

long, long before Joseph of Nazareth, saved his people from starvation during seven years when no rain fell. You know what this means, when no rain falls for a long time. Therefore he was a figure of San José, who provided for Jesus and Mary in those very hard and dangerous first years, and who also provides for Christians who pray to him with confidence. Ah, what is a figure, my boy? Well, for example, if you provide for Soledad, as I know you will, then San José will have been, in a way, a figure of yourself! Do you see?"

He could plainly see that José Vera did not see too clearly. Never again would he touch on that allegory, or any other stretched comparison.

"But, Padre, what is meant by seven fat years and seven lean years?"

"Prosperous years and hard years, my son."

"Seven years of much rain and seven years of no rain?"

"Yes, yes. But they do not have to be exactly seven years each time. They could be two and five, or four and three. (*Mon Dieu*, why did I bring this on myself!)

"Only remember this, José. If you serve the Lord, and are devoted to your namesake, God will take care of you in bad years as well as in good years. Now, go with God, and have the wedding ready for June when I come here again."

The young man smiled contentedly while the Padre hid his own mingled discomfiture and relief under the Mass vestments he was pulling off over his head.

Before asking for Soledad's hand, José did over his
father's little house thoroughly, something the other young
swains of La Cunita, or anywhere else in New Mexico,
would have sneered at as overly particular. Besides repair-
ing roofs and replastering walls inside and out, he remade
the furniture his father had made. The tongues and
grooves had loosened or broken off since his mother passed
away. José re-fitted them and then carved the bedstead,
the clothes chests, the sides of tables and benches, with
the same stiff rosettes and shells that he saw painted on the
altar of San José. Not to be caught short, he built a small
cradle, carved with cherub heads that could be easily mis-
taken for apples, and he also made a little low table with
half a dozen toy chairs to go with it.

Soledad's father and mother put on surprise when José
made his formal plea one bright spring morning. Since he
had no parents to do it for him, nor any relatives like the
other intermarried folk of La Cunita, he brought along as
spokesman an old unkempt fellow by the name of Urbán,
the village midwife's husband. The choice had nothing to
do, in José's mind, with the cradle and toy furniture. It so
happened that Urbán was the only man on hand at the
moment the shy groom had worked up enough courage.
The rest of the townsmen were out working their fields
or looking over their livestock on the prairie.

"*Señor y Señora,*" Urbán began orating through his
bleached and stained shaggy whiskers. "Unworthy though
I am, the honor and pleasure have fallen upon me to
bring you tidings of grievous import and tremendous con-

sequences for the future, which God alone in his temerarious ways can foresee, since there comes a time in the life of male members of the human genus—one worthy sample for whom I speak in the unfortunate circumstances of his being bereft of progenitors to plead for him . . ."

The florid prelude was cut short by the parents' quick acceptance of José, and joyful Soledad was summoned from the kitchen, where she had been spying and listening, to have her moist hand placed in José's with archaic blessings uttered in centuries-old Castilian rhymes that were almost unintelligible from being worn round and smooth at the edges.

The Padre's summer visit came early in June, and La Cunita was ready for him with many baptisms to be performed after the Mass, and some spots to be blessed in the graveyard. He also found the entire apse of the chapel silvery gold with *capulín* blossoms (like lilacs of France, but pale yellow and more delicately fragrant), the native chokecherry that filled a moist ravine next to the pine forest further up the narrow valley. And he was proud to see how charming José and Soledad looked, kneeling before him on the altar step.

The whole village was there rejoicing, as were the dogs which cannot bear a dwelling emptied of all human life, just as they attended as one the four yearly Masses, the fiesta of San José, or the wakes and priestless burials whenever one of the villagers departed from La Cunita for the first (and last) time in his short or long life.

After the nuptial Mass the bridal couple was led to

the bride's home by two musicians, one man sawing away jerkily on a rawhide violin, and his companion strumming a cracked paunchy guitar that seemed to have been sired by a bullfiddle. The cooks had left the chapel early, and the bride's parents had been rushed home before the procession started to receive the wedded pair at their door. There José and Soledad knelt on the threshold to kiss the old couple's leathery hands, which blessed them in turn with the sign of the cross. Then they went in, followed by the elder guests, to partake of a little drink and sweet cinnamon biscuits before being called to the wedding board.

There was no wine, and the Lord was not there, visibly, to fill their waterpots as had happened with similar gentle folks long ago. Here the season was much too brief for grapes, a fruit which only the older folks remembered years back in the valley of the Rio Grande. The small drink offered was sugared water, lime-soured with the crushed green beads of the *lemita* bush, which grew among the scruboaks. There also was another drink, foul-tasting and fiery, which only Urbán, who made it, was able to relish. The tougher males managed to down a small mouthful of it, to be polite to their host and appear strong and brave to their womenfolk.

After sundown everyone followed the musicians to what was called the *sala de fandango*. This was a lengthy old adobe room used now and then for dances. It was roofed over with log beams and a foot of earth, just like the chapel and the dwellings, except that it was in much more need of repair. Against the rear wall a canopied throne had been fixed up with bedsheets and shawls, where the bride and groom were to preside all evening, after they had led the first dance. It was here that it happened.

Earlier in the evening thin streams of fine dry dust had begun sifting down on the necks of dancing couples and of elderly people on benches along the walls. It came from the pounding of running feet above. Boys who were not old or brave enough to take a dancing partner, had propped a ladder outside to chase one another up and down the flat earthen roof. Tired of shooing them away time and again, the older men had resigned themselves to an annoyance which they themselves recalled causing many years before. The fiddle and guitar were still screeching and thumping hours later, the older folks were still prancing and twirling on the hard earth floor, the boys were still running up and down the ladder and stamping all over the dirt roof, when the rotten old beam over the canopy broke in two and let down an avalanche of dusty soil upon José and Soledad.

José was pulled out unhurt, but the longer end of the snapped *viga* had slipped down heavily onto Soledad's lap. Grimy as he was from head to foot, the groom himself carried her to her mother's house like a broken doll, except that she breathed and moaned faintly with pain, and her voice seemed to come from far away.

The fiesta of San José came around once again, and found Soledad motionless in bed at her father's house.

Many weeks later, in June, José brought the first choke-cherry blossoms to Soledad's bedside. For almost the entire summer, last year, she had lain motionless, without knowing that her husband sat every night through at her side, or that during the day her mother and the town mid-wife swathed her hips and thighs with new poultices and bandages. Then she returned, slowly and hesitantly at first, to become aware of José's hands around her own, and by Christmas the midwife proudly predicted that she would be up and dancing with José when the March fiesta of San José arrived once more.

But though Soledad's color came back, and the life in her eyes from a faraway land behind them, her little body from the waist down stayed pinned down by the weight of an invisible *viga*. Because she could now eat and sleep well, the midwife sagely foretold that she would walk home on the day of her wedding anniversary and sleep in the bed that José had carved with shells and flowers.

However, on the day that José came in with the first chokecherry blossoms, Soledad lay bedridden still, sobbing deeply among the pillows. Her mother and father stood gravely by. Urbán was there, too, at the side of his herb-woman, who was also crying to herself, for she had finally admitted the truth to herself and shamefacedly told it to the girl and her parents, little realizing that her restoring of half of Soledad to health had been miracle enough.

Now the midwife said bluntly to José: "She will never

walk again. Her hips have shrunk—like this—like a little boy's. She is your wife, and not your wife."

José halted and stared at the woman. Her quiet voice burst clear into his ears like a shout. It seemed as though he had been living in a dream for twelve months now, and that he really had heard no one speak out loud until this moment.

Soledad's father began shaking him gently. "My son, José, it must be the will of God. Our daughter can stay with us always, her mother and myself, and Urbán's wife to help. But we leave that to your own judgment, son. She is your wife."

"Your wife, and not your wife . . ." José felt Soledad's eyes upon him. They were wet, but still they firmly locked into his own stare and held it. It was the same full look she had given him when the Padre called them man and wife, yet somehow not the same, not quite the same. Or else it was he who was different.

"Let her decide," he stammered at last.

Soledad shook her head. "You are the man, José. You decide."

José gestured, but the words lodged in his throat.

"No, not right away. Come back tomorrow morning," Soledad said, closing her eyes and letting her head sink back into the pillows.

José hung his head for a moment, and then trudged out the door.

No one was in sight the length of the whole street. Most

of the people were out on the fields, plowing, sowing, mending fences and corrals. They were always doing that. He remembered the day Urbán spoke for her hand. Today there was no one to speak to, no father and mother to turn to, the way Soledad could. He found himself by the chapel, not by happenstance as in romances, but by instinct, and went in to kneel before San José. He knelt there for a long time, but said nothing, thought nothing. His mind was numb, his lips were dumb.

And San José himself was no different. The wooden statue stared and stared into space with his even almond eyes outlined with black and white on his narrow yellowish face. His black beard, more like tar dabbed around from ear to ear, made him look more impersonal, as if he did not care about either joy or sorrow. He had stared this way over the crude coffins of José's father and mother, and a year ago over his own head and the white-veiled brow of Soledad. If he would only bow a bit, or shift the tiny Infant from his left arm, or move one of his stiff cornstalk legs and big splayed feet that showed underneath his purple gown. Now he remembered the Padre saying it was a little too short. If he would only shake the tall staff in his right hand and rustle the paper flowers that the women tied to the top of it every feast day.

José did hear a paper rustling in the bare stillness of the chapel, but it was only an angry wasp trapped at one of the windows.

He went home, at last, to find Urbán waiting at his hand-carved table. A jug stood at his elbow. His brown-toothed grin among the mottled red and gray whiskers looked much more human than St. Joseph's. There was a live friendly gleam in his red-rimmed hazel eyes. The older man motioned to the bench, and José sat down beside him.

"Here, this is what you need." Urbán said, leaning closer to offer him a drink. "This is what any man needs. I learned the trick from an *Americano* in Taos, years before you were born, before we came to live here. He was from a place called Kentuck, bless his soul, and he was killed in a brawl. Great man. Do you know that the Indians have had corn for thousands of years, and all they made was cornmeal? Then our own people have grown corn for hundreds of years, and all they could make was cornbread and *posole*. But this grand *señor* from the States knew how to find the very spirit of the corn, the only medicine for a he-man's sickness. Here, take some . . ."

José had pulled back and turned away holding his breath. People had good cause to say that Urbán stank like a dead cow out on the prairie. Outside, the prairie breeze helped to make him tolerable, but folks stole away from his side at fandangos and in the chapel. Thinking it was the jug from which the young man shrank, he urged him on, and José, ashamed of his unkind gesture, took the jug and raised it to his mouth. As if the taste were not torment enough, the large swallow that he hastily downed cut a burning gash all the way down his throat. Coughing and gasping he got up and threw himself face down upon the bed.

Sometime later, José began to notice that the tightness in his head was gone. He felt a knot in his breast becoming untied. Sitting up, he saw that Urbán was gone. But the jug was still there. Yes, there, he thought, was another good friend. Harsh and ill-smelling though it was, like its maker, it had the same understanding heart. And if one swallow could heal the head so quickly, others would reach the heart. Several pulls at the jug later, José felt the room swaying. Then his stomach jumped up as if trying to escape through his mouth. He rushed out retching through the door, and then came back and flung himself upon the bed.

He had lain quiet for some time when the sound of footsteps made him sit up. Thinking it was Urbán who had returned, he called him but got no answer. He could barely see for the throbbing on his pate and temples, as though someone were using his own hammers on them. After he got used to the afternoon glow in his eyes, he kept on frowning and shaking his head at what he saw.

For it was the image of San José standing in the middle of the floor.

What sacrilegious thought had prompted Urbán to play such a prank on him? One did not play with the saints.

"I have come to help my namesake in his troubles," said the little statue.

Its lips actually moved. José caught a glimpse of moist white teeth as it spoke.

"Oh, my head, my head," José moaned to himself. "I will never touch that poison again."

"You say well, my boy. Never do it again."

This time José leaned over closer. It, *he*, had spoken again. And he was smiling, a real fatherly smile, so much like his own departed father's. The straight swaths of black paint that were his beard still looked like black paint, or tar, but the countenance was more human. He was all alive, even though he was no more than three feet high.

"My boy, I heard your silent prayer in the chapel. You have always been a good lad, and I have come to help you. Take Soledad for your wife, José, bring her home with you. Don't you love her any more?"

"But, *Señor San José*, you do know what all this has done to me. Oh, yes, I still love her . . ."

"Then take her, son. And remember that I know, I know perfectly."

The saint began to recall the Padre's yearly talks on his feast, how Joseph himself had been sorely troubled but finally had taken Mary to wife, all for the sake of the Child, and he pointed to the Infant Jesus on his arm.

There shone a light about him when he said this, and the white paper flowers on his staff began to look and smell like real flowers, though what kind, José could not tell.

"Oh, if only I had a child like Him," said José, entranced.

"Let Soledad be your child, as well as your spouse, my dear boy. And also remember that there are lean years for those who serve the Lord, sometimes very lean and hard years; but He also will provide the fat and prosperous ones. Good-by, son."

With this the saint swiveled stiffly toward the door and waddled away like a duck on his ungainly wide feet. Click-clack, click-clack, they went. . . .

José fell back on the bed and did not wake up until next morning.

Soledad was waiting, all cleaned up and propped up among her pillows when José walked in. She knew what he was going to say, and do, from the manner in which he strode across the high threshold, his eyes eagerly seeking hers. His face was pale and drawn, as from sickness, but his eyes were sharp and hearty.

"I am taking you home now," he almost shouted, bending down to kiss her warmly. "You are my wife—and my baby!"

Her mother began to wail with joy, and hugged her son-in-law tight around the waist, while her father embraced his shoulders. The midwife knelt down and kissed his hands. Then, after promises of everlasting help from the parents and the herb-woman, José lifted his wife up, bed-covers and all, and started out for home. The others formed a little bridal procession, marching in time to the music in their hearts. Urbán, the only man on the street, as usual, took off his tattered hat and rubbed his eyes with cracked knuckles. By evening the whole village had gone to the Vera house to wish them health and every good thing.

For more than three years José and Soledad Vera were an unending joy to themselves and to La Cunita. He fashioned big comfortable chairs for her, one before the window in the front room, another in the kitchen, and the third in his workshop, so that she could watch and chat with him as he worked with his tools. From the front window she had a full view of the village, a wooded spur of foothills, and the vast sea of prairie beyond where the billowing clouds formed pictures endlessly.

Folks never tired of seeing José bundling her up carefully on his wagon whenever he had to go out to tend his field or cut timber in the small forest. When they made calls on the neighbors, or joined the villagers in the chapel for rosary or hymns, Soledad made her appearance in his strong arms, and the very sight brought out tenderness from the most hardened.

But Soledad began to grow paler and thinner, too gradually at first for others to see. José had begun to notice, however, a dimming of the sparkle in her eyes, and in her laughter. She wept in her sleep. Moreover, some unthinking housewives had begun telling her how lucky she was in being free of the pains and burdens of having and rearing children, in not having to strain her arms and back day after day in household work. They really were seeking comfort from her, but she took all this for slurs on her not being able to do these very things for her own husband. Then one day José came in with a bruised eyebrow and swollen jaw. He said a horse had thrown him.

But the same women had to tell her the truth not long after.

A pair of young villagers, who had grown to like Urbán's corn whisky, had openly poked fun at José for being only a quarter-husband, and he had been obliged to trounce them.

José and Soledad had their first quarrel when she up-braided him for not telling her the true story.

Something else started bothering José. It began the day he was fixing a cupboard in the kitchen of the young and chubby widow Casillas. Not that anything wrong was said or done. She had merely offered to hold down a shaky board he was sawing, and the board was not too long either. That was all.

It showed that he had been unaware of other women, healthy women, besides Soledad. Now when she slipped into a pouting mood he did nothing to cheer her up, as he had done before. Even the sight of the cradle and toy furniture he had made five years before began to anger him inside, especially since the night he got up to fetch Soledad some water, and skinned his shin on the cradle's edge.

Although he had long known (Urbán had mentioned it) that the general merchant's wife in Las Vegas would pay good money for such objects, José had not thought of sell-ing the cradle and the other pieces until now. In fact, he had never been interested in going to Las Vegas, to see with his own eyes the strange and unbelievable things that Urbán and others of the men talked about. The railroad had reached the town some months ago, a string of great wagons pulled at great speed by a round iron box built like a bison and filled with fire. This he did yearn to see.

Now was the time to get rid of the toys and some other large pieces he had made, for money which was becoming more and more necessary of late in trading for food or fabrics.

José tersely told Soledad what he was doing when he loaded the wagon one evening. Early the next morning he left her at her mother's house and kept on following the twin ruts over the prairie that led but to one place at the end of two days. Once there, he was not disappointed by the noisy monster that hissed from hunched shoulders to rump with mighty snorts of steam; save for the big funnel of a smokestack, it fitted perfectly with Urbán's picture of a buffalo. Then there were other things, too many to dwell upon at once, but none to compare so far with the train at the depot.

Of course, there was the big store, a house of treasure, and no less wonderful were the kindliness of the bald-headed merchant, with a nose that seemed purposely built for his heavy-rimmed spectacles, and his little fat wife with a very pretty white face and glossy black hair, like a blackbird's coat. She gave him a stack of silver dollars for the cradle and small chairs, and ordered some more made. Her husband was more critical of the larger adult furniture, but gave him many more silver dollars, and offered to buy more when he brought them.

While waiting for a passenger train which, the station

agent told him, would arrive late in the afternoon, José stopped at another store, one with very interesting smells. He could not read the sign above the door, but he knew what it was as soon as he went in, again from Urbán's descriptions. There was only the man behind the bar. Behind him was a great big mirror, as big as a lake, which made rows of bottles in front of it appear twice as many as there actually were. This man had a kind face, too. He asked José if he wanted a shot of whisky. Remembering Urbán and his jug, he winced and shook his head. Then some wine?

José had heard how good wine tasted, but the only wine he had ever seen, and from a distance, was the purplish red liquid which the Padre poured into the chalice in the chapel of San José. He pointed to a bottle of the same color, and the bartender poured him a small glassful of burgundy. He liked it. It was like the aftertaste of ripe chokecherries, but *capulín* never rose like a luscious vapor and lingered in one's head. It was a far cry from Urbán's raspy slop. The man said there were sweeter-tasting wines, and José tried the muscatel, then the tokay. Yes, he liked them very much better.

Two women came in and talked briefly with the bartender in a strange language. Before leaving, each one downed a small glassful of amber liquor. What amazed José was not only the assured poise of their husky frames sheathed in black silk, but the fairness of their faces and necks, the golden sheen of their thick hair, like clean pine

shavings. As the man poured José a small glassful of angel-
ica, he told him about these ladies whom the iron bison
had brought.

Their place stood behind the general store, the first
house with a porch, on the street to the left.

José staggered out, not too dizzy in his head, but unable
to control his legs for a while. After he succeeded in tam-
ing them, a masterful feeling welled up in his chest, as
when one brought a wayward team of horses into line.
Yes, palomino horses, with manes like clean pine shavings.
He walked slowly up toward the store and around it. But
instead of taking the left-hand street he wandered to the
right. The first house had a porch, and also a white picket
fence in front—and something else that brought him to a
halt with a most pleasant shock.

It was a little garden of flowers, most of them stalks almost as tall as himself, each hung with rows of paper-like
cups. On some stalks they were red, on others pink, but
most were white. Only they were not paper. José reached
over to touch one and a bee buzzed out. The house door
opened at the same time and a little aged woman came
forth, but not angry like the bee.

"You like my flowers, son," she said.

José grinned and nodded. "I never saw such beautiful
flowers before, except in a dream, once."

That vision of five years ago came back to him with a
sweetness more overpowering than that of the wine. Indeed, it melted away any wine-headiness that remained.

"You know, *señora*," said he, amazed by the memory. "You know, they look just like the staff of Saint Joseph back home, in the chapel of La Cunita."

"That is what our people call them, *varas de San José*," the lady explained. "The *Americanos* who brought them call them hollyhocks."

He did not like the English name. It sounded like Urbán clearing his throat out loud in church. But that did not spoil their beauty for him, or their meaning to himself, so well described by their Spanish name. He next wanted to know if the seeds cost much money. He had plenty of silver dollars now.

The lady laughed. Telling him to wait, she went into the house and promptly returned with a paper sack full of dried pods and seeds, enough to sow a small cornfield. They needed little care, she said, and the second year brought hundreds of flowers, and seeds to throw away.

Clutching the sack to his breast, José thanked the kind woman profusely and went back to the store, where he began picking out dresses and shawls for Soledad and her mother, and new wide-brimmed beavers for Urbán and his father-in-law. And things for the midwife, too. The merchant and his wife tried to steer him away to cheaper and more useful items, but stopped when José began telling them all about Soledad. The merchant's eyes moistened behind the thick quoits of glass perched on his nose, and the lady cooed sweetly while big tears ran down her cheeks. They both fixed up a box of canned and packaged foodstuffs for him besides, and José drove back to La Cunita thinking that his silver dollars had paid for everything he brought along.

Soledad had sunk into a deep dark mood after José left. His taking away the cradle and the children's table and chairs had hurt the most. She was sure that he had done it to spite her. But she began to miss him the very first day, since she had never been without him these five years. By the fourth day she had absolved him of all blame, knowing that it was she herself who had widened the rift between them of late. How to make things right without angering him all over again became her chief worry.

Next day every misgiving vanished, when she saw his wagon draw up to her father's doorway. The look in his face, and the way he leaped down to the ground and then strode over the threshold, recalled that morning when he first picked her up with the bedcovers and carried her home from this very room.

Everyone gasped with awe at the gifts he brought. But Soledad became much more interested in the paper sack full of seeds, for she saw that José prized them more than anything he had ever owned. Her delight when he finished a neat picket fence in front of their home brought his old merry self to full bloom. The following summer the little yard brimmed with big leaves like a dark cabbage patch, but José already saw the bright swaying stalks and knew that Soledad saw them with him. That winter, though, she began to grow visibly paler and thinner, and both knew what it meant.

If only she could live long enough to see the first Saint Joseph's staffs.

She did. It was a dwarf forest of snow-white bells that filled her soul with their own beauty that last June, and with the beauty of the look in her husband's eyes. She used to sit unwearyingly at the window, watching them nod gently in the breeze from the prairie, and they were looking in through the window when José found her dead one quiet day.

He buried her next to his father and mother. There were very few of the people at the funeral, for most of the village folk had left La Cunita, including Urbán and his wife. This past year some tall blond men with jowls like coxcombs had come with long-worded papers from Santa Fe, saying that all the prairie around La Cunita now belonged to them. The inhabitants of La Cunita could no longer graze their cattle and sheep on the land. The sheriff of Las Vegas who came with them sheepishly said that they were right, and nothing could be done about it. After getting a pittance for the plots on which their houses stood, the men began taking their families to Las Vegas. They found steady work right away and began replacing the Chinese coolies in the railroad section gangs.

Then José and the very last remnants also left. Because he was very clever with tools, José was hired to work in the roundhouse, where he became intimate with the once awesome iron buffalos which, like human beings, ran down and needed expert care. He also found a new wife in Las Vegas, a very good woman, most devoted and healthy, who knew how to make the best of his growing wages, which were needed for a family that kept pace with them.

This fine woman also shared his love for flowers, and grew hollyhocks with the reddest blossoms, and also pink ones and white ones. But even the white ones had red and purple centers.

THE COLONEL
AND THE SANTO

THE COLONEL HAD SAID LITTLE SINCE THE DRIVE up to Los Alamos and the return ride down its orange cliff approaches, when the Santa Clara Valley opens up like a panoramic canvas of endless blue sky and bluer sierras, the river course below like a string of emeralds set in silver and displayed on the ruffled fabric of ochre deserts. These ruffles were bluffs and mesas of every shape and hue scattered about for miles and ages.

The Colonel was a landscape painter of sorts as well as an amateur geologist, and therefore interested in bits of history connected with each phase of the landscape. The

driver of the car was keeping him supplied with such items, as though he knew the intimate story of every rock and every turn of the river. He, too, was in military uniform, but wearing the small crosses of a chaplain. His rank was lower as were, decidedly, his age and weight. The olive-drab caps and blouses, and the many-hued campaign ribbons over their hearts, were the single point of resemblance between the two men.

But though they had met for the first time in Santa Fe that morning, they understood each other; that is, the younger man knew what words to use in pointing out a cliff of basalt, or naming the color of a sandstone fault, and finally, after they reached bottom and crossed the river, in recounting the strategy used by a Spanish Captain-General of long ago in dislodging the Tewa Indians from the Black Mesa of San Ildefonso to their left.

This mesa looked like the gray-blue uneven pate of some gigantic elephant, and the Colonel spoke for the first time in twenty minutes. It reminded him, he said, of another bluff on a far Pacific island, as well as the one purpose of this his first visit to New Mexico.

He had forgotten the soldier boy all this while, but now the scape and sky, triggered by the sight of that bluff, brought him back to Cash, especially the unbelievably wide and blue sky. For Cash had always talked with a touch of homesickness about his blue sky back home. He believed the lad now.

"Are you quite sure where Cash's mother lives?" he finally asked, swiveling his big weight toward the driver.

His companion nodded and said they had to go on for several more miles to the east, to the foothills of the great sierras, which now were a deep velvet green. What had appeared like a short skip, when he pointed out the place from Los Alamos, was actually a distance of twelve miles or so.

"If they had dropped that thing a couple of months before they did, Cash wouldn't have died," the Colonel said, after the driver had mentioned Los Alamos. "Poor kid. He would have seen this place, this sky, again."

"You must have really liked the fellow, Colonel, to come all the way out here. He must have been a top soldier."

"Well, yes and no. In fact, he was a poor soldier when you come to think of it, and still he was of the best, the very best. And he was a likeable character. You couldn't stay mad at Cash for long."

"Cash? That's a strange name for a boy from these parts. Was it a nickname?"

"Not that I know of, Padre. That was the name in his file—Cash Atencio. Well, he was in my battalion since the division was activated at the start of the war. He started training with us, and was with us until the day he died. You know how one gets to know and like the men who have been with the outfit for years."

The chaplain nodded.

"And Cash was no ordinary soldier, in the sense that he'd fade in the ranks of a company, or even a whole battalion. From the start I noticed Cash. Besides, he showed signs of leadership and quick judgment in field problems. He got to be a sergeant several times."

"Several times?"

"Yes. I had to bust him down to a buck private on different occasions, and each time he climbed up to corporal, and at last to top sergeant. But then he would get busted again. In fact, he was a private, and I had him for my jeep driver, when they got him."

"Colonel, how could he have been a born leader and a likeable character, and still be such a sad sack?"

"Well, let's put it this way. He had brains and other qualities, but didn't realize it. He had all the makings of a good non-com, and let me say that he had no basically grave faults that would call for court-martial. And he was a very religious guy. Never missed chapel on Sundays, and he used to wear a big five-inch cross, you know—yes, crucifix—on the same chain with his dog-tags. Its weight made it drop out of his fatigue jacket while at work, but I never heard of any soldier kidding him about it.

"But all of a sudden Cash would take off without leave, or he would overstay his furlough without notifying his captain. Or he would get drunk downtown on a couple of beers and wreck up the joint, and then resist arrest when the MP's nabbed him. Each time it was a formal military police charge, and so I had to discipline him. But Cash never got mad or sulked. In fact, it was I who got raving mad when I lectured him and pleaded with him like a father, only to see that he could not grasp what I was driving at. I could not drive into his head the idea of responsibility—that's it, responsibility. And that's what most of these Mexican boys lacked."

The driver colored a trifle but grinned to himself. "Pardon me, Colonel," he said. "But let me inform you that Cash and your other boys from these parts were not Mexican."

The older officer's jaw fell at the unexpected remark.

"New Mexico was a Spanish Colony long before New England, and existed for two centuries and a quarter before there ever was a Republic of Mexico. Hence 'Old Mexico' is a mis-statement. And she belonged to the Mexican Republic for only twenty-five years, while she has been a part of the United States now for a hundred years."

"But the people are part Indian, aren't they? Cash looked a little bit Indian."

"One cannot go by looks alone, sir, especially with the Latin races. But even if Cash did have a remote strain of Indian, which is no disgrace, this does not make him a Mexican. The famed Will Rogers, whom you mentioned this morning as distant kin of yours, was a quarter Indian. Does this make him a Mexican? Of course not. This is because the word 'Mexican' denotes a nationality and a culture, and a very superior one. A citizen of Mexico, whether he be white, red, black, or mixed, is a true Mexican and proud of it. He might make social distinctions, but not racial ones. It is we reputedly democratic Americans who make them, and incorrect ones at that."

"I'm sorry," the Colonel apologized. "You see, that's what I have always heard. Only this morning, at the hotel, a Santa Fe gentleman referred to these people as Mexicans."

The chaplain was laughing. "I am not blaming you, sir, just explaining, just as we were discussing geology, history, and art a while back."

As the Colonel remained gloomily silent, the driver chuckled and spoke again.

"Let's get in a bit of psychology also. It is only here in New Mexico that some people can *think* the word 'Mexican' and at the same time pronounce the altogether distinct word 'Spanish.' It's a hard trick with many a slip. And do you know that we priests are the worst offenders?"

"No!" the Colonel started. "That's strange."

The chaplain could feel that his companion had regained his composure, now that he shared his *faux pas* with others.

The Colonel did feel more at ease now, but at the same time he began wondering if Cash had resented the term. He could not recall a single instance, but it might go some way towards explaining his irresponsible outbursts. The last time was at Seattle, when he almost missed the boat for the islands. Not that he was afraid to go. Cash was afraid of nothing. He simply went off the restricted area, wrecked a small bar and restaurant downtown, and was dragged up the gangplank by the military police at the last moment. From then on Sergeant Cash was a private until the day he died.

That day was a dark and muggy one, just like most days in the tropics during the rainy season, and especially during action. It seemed as though constant artillery barrages and aerial bombings tended to shake the heavens loose. The regiment had been detailed to take the northern tip of the big island, and had done so after almost a week of heavy fighting and mopping up. The regimental commander was killed by a sniper's bullet on the second day, and the Colonel, then a light Colonel, was removed from his battalion to take his place. After the main action was over, he remembered Cash down in the battalion and had him transferred up to regimental headquarters.

"He was a wonderful driver in all kinds of bad roads, including axle-deep mud. Besides, he knew what I wanted without my having to say much. That's the advantage of working and training together for a long time. Cash had done well during combat, his captain told me, and was on the list of those to be recommended for decoration. My intention was to use his driving abilities for the time being, and then restore his sergeant's stripes when the medals were dished out.

"Well, it was one of those muggy days, as I was saying, when I decided to inspect some forward gun positions on the other side of Elephant Butte, a lone mountain bluff on our end of the island. This was the name the men gave it, only they mispronounced the second word. Which made no difference as far as looks were concerned. It appeared very much like that Black Mesa we passed, except that it was all green, the bits of steep ground with grass and brush, the bare rock with lichen. Between us and the bluff lay a couple of miles of dense swampy jungle, not open country like this where you can see a jackrabbit leap and hop for a mile. And the sky was a heavy gray, like lead.

"I was kidding Cash about missing his blue skies as the jeep roared and squirmed over the narrow raised road of black muck, always managing to keep from slipping down among the thick stands of dripping palm and bamboo on either side, when more than a dozen enemy soldiers broke out of concealment and blocked the road ahead. I was sitting in front next to Cash, my adjutant on the seat in back.

"Before either of us could say a word, Cash threw the

jeep in reverse and roared madly backward for several yards, while those monkeys began shooting at us. The adjutant and I just got our guns out of their holsters when we were catapulted head over heels into a murky trench of mud and reeds. Then the jeep roared back on the roadbed and made angrily for the roadblock ahead. It was then that I realized that Cash had purposely dumped us off to carry out a plan of his.

"How he got that jeep to clamber back on the road was miracle enough. How he went through that ambush and past it without getting hit was another wonder. Of course, they leaped aside when he rushed past them. Once beyond them, he stopped the vehicle astride the road, took off the rifle strapped to the jeep's side, and began peppering them, using the jeep as a bunker. The adjutant and I wanted to do our part, but the two pistols were in deep water beyond retrieving.

"I saw them toss grenades at the jeep, and suddenly it blew up with a couple of explosions. By the time the smoke cleared away they had slunk back into the jungle.

"We didn't dare move, without weapons, and we lay still in the reeds and palmettos. One of our patrols had started our way on hearing the shooting, but when they reached us the heavens opened up with bucketfuls. When the storm was over we went cautiously to examine the wrecked jeep. But Cash was not there."

The chaplain's car slowed down, veered off the main road and rolled down a short distance among some clumps of bluish-green sagebrush, to stop before a small adobe house dozing cool and quiet under the glossy umbrella of a giant cottonwood.

"Is this the place?" the Colonel asked, shocked out of the reverie which his narrative had conjured up.

"That's what it said on the mailbox by the roadside," the chaplain answered, going over to knock on the low blue door.

For a spell there was no answer, nor any noise, only the very slight but sharp rustle of big leaves overhead. It was like being in a painting, the Colonel felt. Then the door opened quietly, to frame a young mother with a baby on her arm.

Her long black hair and plain dress were disheveled, and the light skin of her bare arms and face glowed with the clean flush that comes from working over hot water. The child and its dress were spotless. When the chaplain spoke to her in Spanish, asking for Cash's mother, she replied in English, first excusing her appearance, then bidding them come into the house. She was Cash's sister. Her husband was up in the mountains getting wood. Her mother was at the neighbor's down the road. While they made themselves at home she would run down and fetch the old lady.

The Colonel began to feel a strange comfort in the room. He soon found the answer in the wavy floor, which felt like packed earth that was padded over with neat rag-rugs of every size and shape—and in the uneven flow of the white-washed walls from floor to equally uneven cloth ceiling. He had felt the same comfort in a campaign tent; it was the round touch of mother earth, of one's own mother. He was about to expound to his companion about the true functionality and hominess of rounded uneven surfaces, as against unorganic modernistic angles, when an old picture on the end wall caught and held his eye.

"Say! That's the strangest way of dressing Christ on the Cross!" he almost shouted, getting up and pacing over to examine it more closely.

It was a two-foot wooden panel, uneven like the walls, with a few thin cracks running up and down with the grain, which was almost visible underneath the age-darkened pigments. The main figure stood out because of the simple black outlines, without depth, like a child's effort or one of those modernistic French paintings—only not so impudent and glaring. At the foot of the cross were painted six miniature soldiers. The first had a drum, the rest stood at dress parade with their little muskets.

But the main crucified figure, in military uniform like the tiny soldiers beneath, still clamored for an explanation.

The Padre was laughing quietly to himself, and finally began to explain.

"That is not Christ on the Cross, sir, but the figure of a once very popular saint in New Mexico, by the name of San Acacio. Acacio! That explains Cash's name. I'll bet you anything it was his grandfather's name, and his father's also."

The Colonel's face went suddenly drawn and colorless as he leaned for a moment against a rug-covered chest that stood below the picture. When he spoke again his voice was hoarse and trembling.

"This is a most uncanny thing, Padre. I hadn't finished telling you about Cash's death. I said we didn't find his body by the wrecked jeep after the rainstorm was over. But hours later some of our men did find him—like this." And he pointed to the saint.

"He lay face-up on a steep slope of Elephant Hill with arms stretched out, and a bayonet through each hand pinning him to the ground. That crucifix he always wore was hanging out of his open denim jacket. Perhaps it gave those demons the idea. My theory is that they dragged him over to the hill during the storm. I only hope that he was already dead."

He contemplated the painting before speaking again.

"This 'San Cashio' must have been a Spanish officer. He's wearing a colonel's uniform of Spanish troops in the early 1800's—epaulets, black sailor hat of the period, scarlet sash over light blue blouse, and long white trousers stuck in campaign boots. Only the boots are more like a cowboy's."

"They were military boots originally, sir," the chaplain offered, pointing out where a much later hand had drawn curved tops on each boot and added the curlycue decorations affected by Western footwear. No, he further explained to the Colonel, San Acacio was not a colonel in the Spanish army of the early nineteenth century, but this uniform did date the painting itself. It must have been in this Atencio family for three generations or more. San Acacio himself, or St. Achatius, was a Roman army officer of the fourth century, serving in Asia Minor. Because he and his men had become Christians, they were all crucified like their Master. The little soldiers could represent his executioners, or even his own soldiers before they themselves were nailed to crosses.

"And Cash was one of his little soldiers," the Colonel said, pounding his fist forcefully.

Just then they heard footsteps at the door, and turned around to see the young woman with her child. In front of them was a tiny wisp of an old lady in a long black dress. Her small round face, netted with wrinkles, and the clasped hands in front of her small bodice, were browned by thousands of sunlit days. Her white hair was swept back tightly into a neat ball of cotton on the back of her neck. Her large brown eyes were guilelessly clear, like a little girl's, yet rich with the sweet pains of a lifetime bravely borne.

This was what the Colonel saw while the chaplain made the usual introductions and explained the unusual visit, and then proceeded to tell the old woman (all in Spanish) about her son's death in the islands. Meanwhile, the sister in the background was crying softly to herself.

At one moment, when some invisible light suffused the aged mother's features as a quiet smile formed on her lips, the Colonel put his hand on the chaplain's shoulder and interrupted him.

"Padre, be sure not to tell her how we found him."

"But I just did, sir."

The old lady looked up at the Colonel, but spoke to the

chaplain: "Tell the gentleman how proud I am to know that my son died like the Lord and like his patron saint."

With this she took the hand of the Colonel, who had taken out a ribboned medal to pin on her dress, and kissed it reverently. Then she took the decoration from his helpless fingers, glided over to the *santo*, and stuck the open pin in a crack over San Acacio's heart. It covered most of his blue blouse.

AUTHOR'S NOTE

Retablo (*ray-tah-blow*), n. 1. A sacred picture crudely painted on a board. 2. A series of such paintings, also statues, set in panels or niches on a decorated frame to form a reredos or altar-screen.

—UNWRITTEN DICTIONARY OF NEW MEXICO SPANISH

YOU WILL NOT FIND THIS "RETABLO" OF SEVEN panels in some remote chapel in the hills of Talpa or Chimayó, or exhibited in the Taylor Museum at Colorado Springs or the Old Palace of the Governors in Santa Fe. Nor have any of the separate panels been part of the public domain, as in the Brooklyn Museum or the Harwood Foundation at Taos. Much less have they belonged to any of the several private collections throughout the country and, most assuredly, they have never seen handling in a curio shop. The truth is that I filched every bit from the more general domain of New Mexican sky, scape, and village; more particularly, from the shadows cast by firs and piñons at certain hours, from the still air of adobe homes and chapels at dusk. The outlines of each figure are from folks known through the years, the lines on old faces especially. Any resemblance to actual catalogued *retablos* is meant to be that way.

The whole thing is more of a *tableau* (this word is a first cousin to *retablo*) picturing the soul of a simple people at various periods across a couple of centuries. The more or less exact date of each tale appears hidden somewhere in the background of each panel. Hence, this is less a collection of short stories than a running series of accounts about different generations in the same general locale. If the stiff *santos* sometimes step out and move about, quite at home, among the living characters, it is because these folks lived so close to them that they saw and heard them plainly in their life's moment of deepest distress, or else might have seen them.

The tale about the woodcutter and the little angel appeared some years ago in *The Southwest Review* of Dallas, and the tale of the black and white ewes in *New Mexico Quarterly* of the University of New Mexico. The rest have been let out on occasion during the past few years to the Franciscan monthly, *St. Anthony Messenger*, in Cincinnati. But since then the pictures have been done over, a touch here and there, in some cases a total shifting of the plan and figures, as artists sometimes do with their unsold paintings. Having assembled them at last in one reredos, I wish to thank the editors of the publications mentioned for letting me do so, and also Paul Horgan, through the dedication, for showing them to his publisher and to Peter Hurd.

Fr. A.C.

NIHIL OBSTAT:
FR. LAMBERTUS BROCKMANN, OFM
IMPRIMI POTEST:
FR. VINCENTIUS KROGER, OFM
MINISTER PROV. CINCINNATI 10.4.56.
NIHIL OBSTAT: O.A. COGGIOLA. IMPRIMATUR:
✠ EDVINUS VINCENTIUS BYRNE, DD.
ARCHIEPISCOPUS SANCTAE FIDEI: 11.26.56